MW01224257

Damage Control

Books by Michael Bowen

The Washington Crime Stories
Washington Deceased
Faithfully Executed
Corruptly Procured
Worst Case Scenario
Collateral Damage
Damage Control

The Thomas and Sandy Stories
Badger Game
Fielder's Choice
Act of Faith

The Rep and Melissa Pennyworth Mysteries
Screenscam
Unforced Error
Putting Lipstick on a Pig
Shoot the Lawyer Twice
Service Dress Blues

Writing as Hillary Bell Locke

The Cynthia Jakubek Legal Thrillers
But Remember Their Names

The Jay Davidovich Mysteries
Jail Coach

Featuring Jay Davidovich and Cynthia Jakubek
Collar Robber

Damage Control

A Washington Crime Story

Michael Bowen

Poisoned Pen Press

First Edition 2016

10 9 8 7 6 5 4 3 2 1

Library of Congress Catalog Card Number: 2015957978

ISBN: 9781464206054   Hardcover
      9781464206078   Trade Paperback

Poisoned Pen Press
6962 E. First Ave., Ste. 103
Scottsdale, AZ 85251
www.poisonedpenpress.com
info@poisonedpenpress.com

Printed in the United States of America

For Jade and Hailey, with deep affection and high hopes.

Acknowledgments

Special thanks to Murphy Gadlock for helpful and constructive insights into the theory and practice of political life in contemporary Washington, and into the general ethos that prevails there. "Murphy Gadlock" is a pseudonym for a seasoned observer of the Washington scene who doesn't want his or her real name to be disclosed. It is also an anagram for "grumpy old hack," but that's a coincidence, not a clue.

Principal Characters in the Story

Josephine ("Josie") Robideaux Kendall

Raphael ("Rafe") Kendall, Josie's husband

Evangeline Barry Robideaux, Josie's mother

Darius Zachary Taylor Barry, Josie's uncle

Seamus Danica, Josie's boss

M. Anthony ("Tony") York, Josie's lawyer

Jerzy Schroeder, aspiring crony capitalist, potential client of Josie

Ann DeHoic, Schroeder's ex-wife

Danny Klimchock, former business associate of Schroeder

Sanford Dierdorf, successful crony capitalist

Theo McAbbott, retired FBI agent, thrillers author, client of Rafe

Reporters/political commentators/media types:
    Terry Fielding
    Lizzie Nygren
    Major Fitz
    Matt Crisscuts

Author's Note

Damage Control is a work of fiction. It is not a *roman à clef* featuring characters who are thinly disguised versions of actual elected officials, staffers, activists, reporters, lobbyists, fund-raisers, executive branch appointees, or other players in Washington, D.C. To anyone in any of those categories, all I can say—and I mean this in the gentlest possible way—is that you aren't in here, so don't kid yourself. Aside from St. Monica and well-known political personalities mentioned in passing under their actual names, I invented the characters all by myself and I made up out of whole cloth the events described. Any resemblance, actual, apparent, or perceived, between those characters, descriptions, and events and what passes for the real world in Washington these days is accidental and unintended.

"A damage control strategy that hasn't succeeded in thirty days has failed."

—Murphy Gadlock[1]

---

1 See Acknowledgments.

Chapter One

"My blouse is evidence. How was *your* day?"

"Better than that." Rafe sounded wry and unruffled. As usual.

"You got my text?" *The one I sent almost four hours ago*—Nd 2 tlk ASAP.

"Yeah…spent almost the whole day with Theo. Just picked it up. Sorry."

"It doesn't really matter, I guess. I couldn't have taken your call while I was talking with cops anyway, and for most of the drive back into the District I've been on the phone with Tony." M. Anthony York is my lawyer. Goes by Tony when Democrats hold the White House.

"We should talk, but not over cell phones. How soon will you be home?"

"Twenty minutes." I checked my watch. "Maybe fifteen."

"I'll have your martini ready."

Rafe was right, of course. So *not* cool to jabber over the air about Jerzy Schroeder being dead before I heard the shot that killed him. Blood and brain tissue spattered my DKNY blouse, and only a split-second later had I heard the *ka-pow!* and pivoted back-left to watch in nauseated shock as Jerzy's body jerked forward and fell. The muzzle velocity of a hunting rifle versus the speed of sound, four-hundred-fifty yards, do the math.

I hadn't knelt to check for signs of life or cradle what was left of his head. I'd hauled ass. Flight or fight, flight wins.

I'd called nine-one-one from behind an elegantly curved marble bench ten yards away, near Jerzy's fish pond—by then his heirs' fish pond. After I'd reported gunfire and a corpse *chez* Schroeder, twenty miles west of Annapolis, the dispatcher had asked if I was okay.

"Scared and shocked but not physically injured."

"Please stay on the line until police arrive."

No way, Cinderella. She'd gotten my name—Josie Kendall—and should consider herself lucky she'd gotten that.

"You're breaking up."

I punched off. Called my boss. Never let anyone beat you to the man with bad news. Told him prospects for a Schroeder buy-in had just dropped to zero. Then I'd called Rafe. Then I'd texted Rafe. Then cops were there.

Cop-chat is not bad as pains-in-the-butt go except that, what with digging up a replacement blouse and the bathroom sponge-off they'd grudgingly allowed, it had taken over two hours. The questions were roughly what you'd expect, starting with why I'd happened to be four feet from Jerzy when he'd bought it.

"We were talking about a nonprofit I work for called Majority Values Coalition. I'm in development."

"Fund-raising, in other words."

"That's part of it."

"What's the rest of it?"

"Ideas."

"First time you'd ever seen the decedent out here?"

"No. I'd come out here to see Jerzy—Mr. Schroeder—at least twice a week for the last month or so."

"He must have had some really interesting ideas."

No, he had some really interesting money.

"He was a very thoughtful man. He'll be missed." Oops. Less than an hour earlier he definitely had *not* been missed.

"Do you know of anyone who might have wanted to kill him?"

"No."

I could count at least three. But I didn't want Jerzy's enemies on my tail—especially whichever one had just taken him out. So track down the bad guy yourself, Kojak. I'll be right over here, staying alive.

I told Rafe the story while I sipped the vodka martini he had ready for me. He served it to me with his customary aplomb, not a single hair in his perfect white mane ruffled, every syllable off of his silver tongue appropriately concerned but untinged with panic. At fifty-one Rafe is twenty-four years older than I am, but the D.C. consensus is that I was damn lucky to get him—not vice versa. Together five years now, married four of them. I'm pretty sure he's never cheated on me—not even a weekend romp—so the consensus is probably right. I raised my glass to the ten-foot-two-inch stuffed polar bear gracing our foyer.

"Here's to you, Strom." Rafe had named the bear postmortem after Senator Strom Thurmond—post the bear's mortem, not Thurmond's.

"So who did it?" Rafe's question.

"Best guess is his ex-partner, Danny Klimchock. He and Jerzy had a thing going with some kleptocrats in Russia a few years ago. Klimchock spent some unpleasant time as Putin's guest after the deal cratered. When he finally got back here Jerzy gave him his one-million-dollar share of what he'd salvaged from their venture. Klimchock said that was about ten million light. They haven't exchanged holiday cards since."

"Any other candidates?"

"A mobbed-up judge in Massachusetts who blamed Jerzy for getting his kid crosswise of an Assistant United States Attorney. Junior got off with community service and a good talking-to, but his Honor might have reverted to his Celtic roots anyway. And then of course there's Sanford Dierdorf, whose federal subsidy for solar power development would go away if the finesse with the Energy Department that Jerzy was talking to me about had come off."

Rafe puffed contemplatively on a cigar. He gazed through the window. Didn't say a word. I wiggled my fingers at him and he offered me a hit on the stogie. I loved it. That's the problem with giving up cigarettes: you start cultivating bad habits. He spoke up.

"There are only three times you smoke cigars: New Year's Eve, when you're with your mom, and when you're stalling. It's mid-July and mom is two thousand miles away, so what's the deal?"

I blushed. "Tony thinks the cops will suspect you. He says they'll assume Jerzy and I were having an affair and that you found out and got all old-school about it."

"Tony isn't the savviest shyster Yale Law ever sent down I-95, but he's probably right. Cops are like editors—they're paid to have dirty minds." Rafe waited three beats for me to confirm or deny infidelity; when I did neither, he continued. "That probably explains the unmarked car with a Maryland government license plate that's driven past our house three times and just pulled up at the curb. Two cheap suits with 'cop' written all over them. Salt and pepper."

From eighty feet away, looking at guys still in their car, Rafe had hit the bull's-eye. Ebony from D.C. and ivory from Maryland. Out of the car and almost thirty yards later, on our porch, they told Rafe about Jerzy's murder and said they had some questions. Neither of them mentioned a warrant. They noticed Strom right away. The white one asked who'd nailed him.

"I did," Rafe said, "over fifteen years ago. Winchester bolt-action three-oh-eight."

"You still have the rifle?"

"Nope. Sold it a few years ago. I don't care what the Supreme Court says, it's too much hassle possessing a firearm in D.C. Besides, I haven't gone big game hunting for ten years, maybe more. Peepers are way south of what you need for that. So the rifle was just a relic of youth, and what's the point? Might be able to dig up the paperwork, if it would help."

"It would help."

"This may take a while. You can come along if you like."

Rafe headed upstairs. The black detective went with him. The white one turned toward me as soon as we couldn't hear Rafe's steps on the stairs.

"What does Mr. Kendall do for a living?"

"He's a literary agent and a consultant." A bit telegraphic. Rafe sells other people's books to publishers and he consults with people willing to pay for his conversation, but his real *métier* is navigator. Out of the thousands of J.D.s and B.S. (Economics) and A.B./M.A. (Political Science) types who come to Washington every year, he spots a few who, down the road a bit, might be ready to make a power move, sail through the dark and stormy seas of politics from Congressional staffer or underpaid blog content provider to regular panelist on a cable news show or cabinet-level senior aide or campaign consultant. In D.C., this is called "monetizing your resumé." Rafe does this for two reasons. First, folks who bring the move off big-time write books that generate huge advances, even though they're read mostly by people who look in the indexes for their own names. Second, Rafe gets his calls returned when he wants those upwardly mobile types to arrange a meeting for someone with their bosses or sometimes even themselves. Various someones pay Rafe money to do this.

In answering the detective, though, I stuck with the short version. Instead of drilling down he moved on.

"How are you and Mr. Kendall getting along in your marriage?" Just like that, with all the finesse of a corporal telling his favorite whore about the clap test.

"Pure bliss." I hope that came across as *Fuck you,* 'cause that's what I was going for. Pretty much true, though. Rafe is a long way from blue pill territory, and he could charm the socks off a process-server. The thrills aren't the same after five years, but that's life. At that point I viewed my little tumble with Jerzy as just a thing. Jerzy was basically a gangster—a rich gangster who knows wine vintages and can read music is still a gangster. A girl likes a little *frisson* of bad-boy excitement now and then. Danger as aphrodisiac.

After a good twenty minutes Rafe and the black detective came back down. The latter held a piece of stiff paper still showing tri-fold creases. Rafe looked almost childishly pleased with himself.

"I can't believe I found that thing! Here, let's make a copy on the printer. You'll want to keep the original, right?"

"Right."

With a sheepish, technophobe grin Rafe accepted the document from the detective and handed it to me. I used the printer/FAX/copier next to Rafe's computer in the study to duplicate it. Interesting. Hand-printed. Dated three years and two months before. Winchester 308 b/a—bolt-action? must be—hunting rifle. Serial number *lotsofdigits*. Sold to Alphaeus Bittenwald of Mason-Dixon Heritage Firearms for one-hundred-twenty dollars cash at a gun show in Norfolk, Virginia. The black detective had come along to keep me company, so I just handed the original back to him. By the time we returned, the white detective had started rolling out what had to be the money question for Rafe.

"Just out of curiosity, how'd you spend your time today?"

"With Theo McAbbott in McLean, Virginia."

"You say that name like you think I should know it."

"If I were doing my job right, you would." Rafe flashed his world-class self-deprecating grin. "Used to be an FBI agent, now he writes thrillers. *Ducks in a Row* about five years ago, big debut hit, and then *Knuckle Rap* oh, when was that? Year before last, I guess. Pretty good yarns. I spent all morning and half the afternoon with him, helping him polish some rough edges off his next entry."

If the cop knew much about literary agents this might have come across as a little labor-intensive for a member of the guild. Made sense to me, though. *Ducks in a Row* had indeed done pretty well. *Knuckle Rap*, however, hadn't exactly kept George Pelacanos awake at night. So I could see where a little extra effort might be in order for the upcoming title, lest McAbbott's third be his last.

"With any luck," the detective said, "we can verify that location from your cell phone."

"Right here?" Rafe shook his head at the wonders of technology as he unholstered his iPhone 6 and handed it over.

"Should take five or ten minutes."

It took seven. USB cord in a portable PC, beeps and clicks, exit cops with thank-yous and handshakes. Rafe watched their car pull away, then turned to me.

"We'd better get to work."

"Yep."

Chapter Two

"Strike 'police officials.' Insert 'law enforcement authorities.'"

"Right. 'Law enforcement authorities have asked Ms. Kendall not to comment further, pending completion of the investigation.'"

"How about 'while the killer is still at large'?"

His Bic poised over a legal pad on his lap, Rafe considered the idea. Then he shook his head.

"No. Melodramatic. Like a *New York Post* headline. Just 'while the investigation is under way.'"

"I agree." This came over speaker-phone from Seamus Danica, my boss. He definitely had a vote. "Read the whole thing."

"'Official sources confirm that Josephine Kendall, senior development director for the Majority Values Coalition [D.C. address and phone number and link to website] was unharmed this morning in the ambush slaying of entrepreneur/environmental activist Jerzy Schroeder on his Maryland farm. Ms. Kendall, who was talking with Mr. Schroeder when a concealed rifleman killed him with a single shot from several hundred yards away, reported the crime to investigators. Law enforcement authorities have asked Ms. Kendall not to make further public comment while the investigation is under way.'"

"Outstanding." Seamus again, who's fluent in hype.

"Okay, who puts it out?" Rafe asked.

"Zap it over here and I will," Seamus said. "That way they'll think we're stonewalling to keep the focus off MVC instead of off Josie."

I'd known the answer before Seamus had given it and I'd been keypunching diligently throughout the conversation, so it was already set to go.

"In cyber-space," I told him one click later.

"See you tomorrow morning. Looks like we have a million-dollar hole to fill."

"Right." Activist fund-raising is an unsentimental business. Seamus hung up. Rafe looked at me.

"Okay. Now comes the hard part."

Rafe and I had had the same thought from the moment our front door closed behind the cops. For them this was a murder investigation. For Rafe and me, it was a damage-control problem, like having one of your ambassadors killed in a terrorist attack that some numbnuts called a spontaneous riot would present if you were the Secretary of State, or having DUI documentation for your candidate pop up in a presidential campaign if you were the campaign manager.

Whipping out a no-further-comment media release was the first damage-control baby step—the equivalent of finding Normandy on a map if you're planning the D-Day invasion. Now to the real work.

Job-one: Get ahead of the curve and stay there. Get the story out, which Seamus was now doing. After the media whores got the we-can't-talk release, start talking—but to the right whores, and without attribution. Job-three will be to control the narrative. That brings us to Job-two: Come up with a narrative to control. I went first.

"Klimchock did it?"

"We can't commit to that yet." Rafe shook his head. "For all we know he's dead or in prison somewhere."

"Right. But if we're not ready to put our money on Klimchock, we sure can't throw one of the other two under the bus."

"True. How about going at it from the opposite direction? Schroeder was a shadowy guy, right?"

"Sure was." I settled back in my chair and told myself not to think about cigarettes. "Got real rich real quick trafficking in stuff that's legal but attracts a dubious crowd. Conflict minerals. Gray market oil. Cash stashed off-shore."

"Any drug cartels or terrorist groups in the background?"

"I doubt it. He was too smart for that, and did just fine without them. Vague rumors about brokering sexual tourism years ago, when he was just starting out in the thug business, but even the worst stories don't say he was a pimp or a consumer. Just a middleman."

"How about grown-up sex?"

"Non-starter. Liked girls, plain vanilla, didn't roll with pols. Divorced for three years. Must have had a high-class call-girl on speed-dial, but who cares?"

"The sexual tourism stuff is provocative even if it's just rumors," Rafe said. "How about something really creepy, like, oh, a private island crawling with cute munchkins where he could take celebrities and influential ex-office holders?"

"No. Jerzy was a Republican."

"Deviant sex is bipartisan."

"As Barney Frank once said to Larry Craig," I agreed, nodding gamely, "'we're on the same page.'"

Rafe favored me with a withering eyebrow.

"That's right, you spend half your time with people who think gay sex is deviant, don't you?"

"Welcome to my world."

"If he didn't have politicians in his pants, how about in his pocket?"

"He spread campaign contributions around in the usual savvy way. Middle seven figures."

"Hence your interest in him."

"Hence my interest in him. MVC had the hots for a piece of that pie."

Pensive pause from Rafe. Thoughtful nibble on the cap of his Bic. I had to wait seven seconds for the next question.

"What would Schroeder have been investing in if he'd sent Majority Values Coalition a check?"

"Delete subsidies for a solar power start-up that's gone six years without starting up and switch the cash to a wind-power thing that Jerzy had some high rollers salivating over. Dierdorf, the guy I mentioned this afternoon, is the solar power honcho. If Jerzy had brought off the switch it would have busted his chops."

"Yeah," Rafe said, drawing the word out, "but risks like that are just part of the Washington game. Some days the eagle flies and some days the eagle shits. Assassination isn't a standard lobbying ploy."

"Neither is threatening criminal prosecutions, but that's what Jerzy had in mind for Dierdorf. He was trying to goose the Department of Energy into an audit—maybe even a full-scale investigation."

Rafe nodded in decisive satisfaction as he scribbled on a legal pad. No question about it: threatening the wrong guy with a close look at the Federal Sentencing Guidelines could get your head ventilated in a big damn hurry.

"Okay," he said, "first cut: Jerzy Schroeder was an entrepreneur with a passion for anonymity, a talent for making money in unconventional ways, and a contact list full of people who don't belong to the Rotary Club. His universe featured sharp elbows and a survival-of-the-fittest mentality, with the standard-issue murky, nameless, but vaguely menacing East Europeans, Russians, and Central Asians floating around just out of sight. Odds are he flew a little too close to the flame and one of them clipped him. How about that for a narrative?"

"Like it, except for the mixed metaphor. But we're going to need at least one specific example that whoever we leak to can sink their teeth into so that they feel like real reporters."

"'*Whom*ever we leak to,'" Rafe whispered, in retaliation for the mixed-metaphor crack. "You're right. Where do we get that?"

"*We* don't get it anywhere. *I* get it tomorrow from MVC's pitch-file."

"Do you think Seamus will be on board?"

"He may be on board without knowing it, but he'll be on board."

Rafe put his pad down on his chair's oversized wooden armrest. He leaned forward. His hazel-brown eyes dripped with tender concern that struck me as completely genuine. For a second or two I felt like shit.

"One implication of our narrative will be that MVC was after money that was tattletale gray even if it wasn't outright dirty."

"When it comes to money, we don't discriminate on the basis of color."

"But you can't say that out loud. You have a good Washington gig, honey—and you could lose it."

"I'm probably toast anyway." I shrugged as I imagined Tammy Wynette belting out "Stand by Your Man" in the background. "Let's learn a lesson from George W. Bush and handle this one war at a time."

"Very good." Rafe slapped his thighs. "We have a plan."

Damage Control Strategy, Day 1

(the first Thursday after the murder)

Chapter Three

You don't go after a million bucks from someone without a detailed pitch-file. MVC had one on Jerzy. It held the material that Seamus' crew of "excellent nerds," so named in homage to Lee Atwater, had assembled from every accessible data source on Earth, and some not so accessible, to help us shape our approach to Jerzy and then close the deal once we had his interest. Excellent nerds are by nature non-discriminating. Their theory is that you can't read it if you don't have it, but you can skip it if you have it and it doesn't help, so they include everything they can get their hands on. That's why I seldom bother with even ten percent of the stuff they rake up. Now, though, I needed media bait, so I'd be digging deeper.

It took less than half an hour the next morning to turn up a pretty good candidate: brokering the sale in China of Lexus cars bought in the United States. Apparently you can sell a Lexus in China for four or five times what U.S. dealer cost is. I assume you have to grease some palms at the Chinese end to get the things into the country, but Jerzy earned his skim by getting the cars from the inventories of American Lexus dealers to loading docks in Long Beach. After that it was somebody else's problem.

You need a Jerzy for the U.S. part because Lexus frowns on having cars delivered to America sold to people who don't know any college fight songs. Hence, the scam requires a little paperwork—a certificate of title here, a bill of lading there—and

Jerzy ate forged documents for breakfast. You also need dealers who'll play dumb. Being a little short of ready cash can make people play flat-out moronic. Jerzy had a talent for coming up with people who were short of ready cash.

You could call all this fraud if you wanted to get tight-assed about it, and Lexus had found a United States Attorney in the Midwest who was downright constipated. He'd gone after the U.S.-based Asian contacts and the saps in the dealerships, but he apparently hadn't come across Jerzy's fingerprints. Yet. That was good enough for a running start on Jerzy as a smoothly suave rogue who fell in with bad companions.

Seamus picked that moment to walk into my office. He sported his customary stringy gray-silver comb-over that somehow looks puckish instead of dorky, sparkling blue eyes that always seem alert, and round face that doesn't show the tank-car-load of Jameson's he's put away over his fifty-nine years. I hadn't told him about digging up Jerzy's past to take the heat off Rafe, so I tried not to look guilty. I've had a lot of practice.

"We may have a lead on filling that million-dollar hole," he said.

"Who?"

"Schroeder's ex-wife—fascinating lady named Ann DeHoic."

"Never heard of her. Fascinating how?"

"Fascinating the same way Schroeder was." That would be money. "Plus, even though you haven't stumbled over her, she doesn't share his aversion to the limelight. Shows up in boldface more than occasionally on page 6 of the *New York Post*. Known in New York, Paris, and Geneva as 'the gray lady.'"

"New York, Paris, and Geneva—no wonder I've missed her. Those aren't TMZ-type places. The plutocrat gossip I traffic in is more Sunbelt-oriented. They have a lot higher ratio of MVC types down there."

"Good thing you're a quick study, then. She'd like to meet you."

I asked the questions that a senior development director with a million-dollar shortfall has to ask in this situation. "Where and when?"

"Outside Brookings at one-thirty."

Seamus couldn't have surprised me more if he'd said outside Lenin's tomb. The Brookings Institution on Massachusetts Avenue in northwest D.C. is where good Democratic policy wonks go when they die. Its amply credentialed denizens generate earnest, carefully researched, closely reasoned reports on head-scratchers like sovereign debt crises and logistical constraints complicating coordination of international efforts to enforce oil-trading sanctions and…Huh? Excuse me? Oh, sorry, I must have nodded off there for a second. Point is, someone—*anyone*—who had an appointment inside that place wanting to meet me would be like Chief Justice Roberts seeking a hook-up with Perez Hilton. At one-twenty-five p.m., though, I stood outside the Brookings Institution, feeling like a high school senior hoping the prom limo would show up on time.

I had briefed myself on Ann DeHoic by blitzing through a thumb-drive Seamus had tossed me on his way out of my office. She'd gone through two husbands before Jerzy: one a Swiss national when she was twenty, formally annulled shortly after her twenty-first birthday; and the other, when she was twenty-four, to a guy whose name looked Russian to me. That one ended in divorce when she was twenty-eight.

No kids with either of those husbands or with Jerzy. The hearsay, though, was that she'd tried hard for a baby with her second husband, including intensive fertility treatments, and come up empty. *Barren*. A biblical curse. That produced a pang in my own breast. I knew Rafe wanted a rug-rat or two, and so did I, but we hadn't gotten below the fifty-thousand-foot level on that yet and the window figured to close for us in five years at most. No way a guy in his mid-seventies could ride herd on the bundles of mid-adolescent attitude and cussedness that my genes figured to produce. There was no reason to doubt my own fertility, but you don't really know until you try. Had DeHoic taken the bad news with philosophical resignation? Or had it maimed something inside her that shrinks have a name for and anatomists don't? Or was she somewhere in between?

High school at a Swiss *lycée* with a pricey-sounding name. Studied art history at Brown but left early in her junior year, around the time of marriage number one, and never bothered to finish her degree. Occasional gigs with art museums in Europe and Asia—nothing you could call a career, though. Parents both dead before she turned thirty. No dope about the size of her trust fund or payouts under pre-nups, but I was betting the only coupons she clipped were on bonds, not supermarket advertising supplements.

As Seamus had said, her name showed up now and then in East Coast gossip columns. Here's something interesting about that part: nary a word out of her mouth. The closest any scribbler ever came to quotation marks in writing about her was a crack in *Time* magazine from a French actor whose name I didn't recognize. He'd shacked up with DeHoic during the Cannes film festival one summer between the Russian and Jerzy, but the tryst had an early end tumultuous enough to get the attention of *Time's* stringer. According to him, the actor had said, "Any male who could spend twenty-four hours with that Yankette without smacking her at least once is either a weakling or a saint." I suspect that the politically incorrect epithet *Time* had euphemized into "weakling" was the one that got a Fox News anchor suspended for using it on the air to describe President Obama.

Chapter Four

I recognized DeHoic the second I saw her strolling out of Brookings' main entrance. Blonde/blue, five-six, one-twenty stark naked if I'm any judge (I am), thirty-six, both age *and* breasts, little tiny bit of work done on the outside corners of her eyes but very subtle, makeup, low-key and perfectly applied.

No mystery about the gray-lady nickname. White cotton Oxford-cloth blouse, but everything else she wore was perfectly matched gray—a little darker than dove but at least three shades short of charcoal. Pumps, skirt, jacket—this is Washington, D.C. in the middle of July and she's wearing a *jacket* with her outfit—hat somewhere between 1950s stewardess and 1990s female midshipman, and dress gloves. She carried the gloves in her right hand instead of wearing them. Louis Vuitton purse also gray. And it all matched. Even the gloves.

"Good afternoon. I'm Ann DeHoic. You must be Josie Kendall." East Coast accent but more Philly than NYC, with a little hint of that Swiss finishing school.

"Yes. Delighted to meet you." We shook hands.

A Mercedes S550 purred up to the curb. Gray. Matched DeHoic's outfit. Seriously. A chauffeur in black livery with red and gold trim popped out to open the rear door for us. His gray uniform must have been at the cleaners.

We slid in. The car started rolling toward DuPont Circle. DeHoic extracted a silver cigarette case from her purse, opened it, and held it out to me. I took one. Snap judgment. Good call. She got one for herself and lit them both with a Piaget lighter that probably cost half as much as my first year in college.

"Jerzy said you don't smoke."

"Basically smoke-free for two years now, but I have a what-the-Hell cigarette every now and then."

"Good for you. Smoking can be companionable, don't you think?"

"Yes."

DeHoic produced an elegant smoke stream at a forty-five-degree angle toward the car's open sunroof, followed by that look of perfect, eyes-closed contentment that confirmed smokers get from the first puff. Then she met my eyes.

"Whoever said politics is show business for ugly people never met you. Your photo on the MVC website is attractive, but it doesn't do you justice. There's something quite striking about you—an *éclat* that the picture doesn't capture."

I inclined my head modestly to acknowledge the compliment, and unconsciously touched the bas-relief St. Monica on the ivory brooch I always wear. Photographers who could do me justice charge more than Seamus would pay for anything short of circus sex with an A-list trio.

"Your hair isn't dyed, is it?" She sounded surprised.

"Nope. Creole mom plus Cajun dad equals jet black and glossy. Same with the complexion that makes me look like I'm just back from spring break in Fort Lauderdale even at Christmas parties."

"New Orleans?" she asked, nodding.

"Baton Rouge." I gave it the Creole pronunciation, closer to French than English. "Carondelet Academy. Started every class with a prayer, and the senior final examination rooms had smoking and non-smoking sections."

"Then on to LSU, I'm guessing."

"Tulane." Apparently she hadn't exactly obsessed over my capsule bio on the website. "Majored in Communications slash Public Policy."

"When did you come to Washington?"

Interesting question. The summer after I turned fifteen my uncle, Darius Zachary Taylor Barry, decided that a summer political job in Baton Rouge would be a mite fast for me. I was still learning multiplication tables when the Monica Lewinsky scandal broke, but as best I can remember no one in Baton Rouge could figure out for the life of them what the fuss was all about. So he pulled a string here and there and set me up with an internship in D.C. instead.

I know Monica turned "intern" into a locker-room leer, but the gig Uncle D finagled for me was the real deal: actual work, and none of it required knee-pads, thank you very much. Staff of the Subcommittee on Sea and Ocean Law of the House Judiciary Committee. *Yawn*, right? Didn't care. I was in the game, a D.C. insider—on the far outside fringe of that self-important club, maybe, but a member all the same.

Loved every second of it: every quorum call, every sort-of-famous face in the elevators, every sly Beltway joke that none of my Carondelet classmates would have gotten. Loved knowing that Senator Charles Grassley, a rock-ribbed Republican from America's heartland, nevertheless thought that "fraudster" should be the collective noun for government contractors; that Chelsea Clinton enjoyed an occasional cigarette and every reporter in town knew it and none of them would ever write a word about it lest their bosses get a nastygram up the keester from one of Hillary's enforcers; that Grover Norquist, the anti-tax maven heading up Americans for Tax Reform, carried his own salt-shaker in his right trouser pocket when he ate out so that he wouldn't have to rely on restaurant salt. I even loved knowing that the Budget Reconciliation Bill was going to pass fifteen minutes before CNN knew it. Bitten by the bug for sure. In September, my body headed back to Baton Rouge, but my heart never left Washington. I went back every summer and most term breaks. At Tulane, I gave up nine months in Paris so that I could spend my junior year in Washington instead, getting college credit for working with green- and tan-covered government reports in places that didn't resemble the Louvre.

So if I'd said that I'd been in Washington for ten years, it would have been a kind of truth. Having tabbed DeHoic for more of a literalist, though, I kept it concrete and told her I'd gotten my first full-time Washington job right out of Tulane, on the staff of a western Congressman named Temple.

"That's a lovely brooch."

"Thank you." I realized that I must have touched it again—and DeHoic had apparently noticed. "My Mama gave it to me when I graduated from Carondelet." I still remembered Mama's little speech on the occasion: "*Josephine, you aren't a thief, you aren't a bully, and you aren't a snitch, so I guess your papa and I did something right bringing you up. But you are a rascal and a scamp. I couldn't bring myself to beat it out of you when I had the chance, and before I knew it you were too old for the fouet. So I guess I'll just turn you over to Saint Monica. When she was in her early teens, she'd slip down to her papa's cellar and sneak some wine every chance she got, so that makes her the patron saint of scamps and rascals.*"

A nod, and DeHoic got down to business.

"How much was your company hoping to get from Jerzy?"

"A million. To start. Dollars, not euros."

"What was this million supposed to buy? And *don't* bother telling me Jerzy gave a rat's ass about conserving America's vital natural resources."

Whoa. I decided my own cigarette was feeling neglected, so I gave it some attention. Then I responded.

"Why would I tell you that?"

"Depends on how much you want the million dollars."

That would be—a lot.

"Okay," I said. "My job was the part of the iceberg above the water."

"You mean the cover story."

"If you like." I shrugged. "Jerzy supposedly had investors cautiously interested in a wind-power boondoggle if Jerzy could swing a federal subsidy for it. What with sequestration, there's no new money from the government for anything except bombing terrorists these days, so we'd have to pull a switch-out."

"Whom were you thinking of switching out?"

I took seven seconds off my life, or whatever a serious puff costs you.

"We're now officially above my pay grade. Have to talk to my boss."

She nodded with no hint of irritation.

"When you talk to your boss, tell him I want to deal with you, not him. I'm thinking of engaging MVC to carry on the noble work Jerzy was doing. Admiration for his fighting spirit blah-blah-blah. A million is too much but I could see going two hundred thousand—if I like what I find when I audit the file. By 'the file' I mean the entire file: the original and all copies, digital and paper."

"Got it." *You want to buy the pitch-file from us and create a client relationship so that we can't sell information to anybody else.* "Just out of curiosity. I have a healthy level of self-esteem, but why are you so anxious to work with me?"

She politely completed an exhalation before turning her head toward me. She smiled.

"Because once a girl's been fucked by Jerzy Schroeder, she knows what getting fucked is. I've found that to be useful knowledge for people I work with."

Chapter Five

"So why is she insisting on working with you?" Seamus' question.

"Promote gender diversity, sisterhood is powerful, we gals have to stick together—that kind of thing. Or so she said."

"Well *that's* bullshit. What do you think the real reason is?"

"Just guessing, I'd say she thinks Jerzy and I were sleeping together."

"Were you?"

"Anything for the team, Coach."

Seamus sucked on a Marlboro red in casual violation of a D.C. ordinance.

"Why would that put you at the top of her list instead of the bottom?"

"What's at the top of her list is motivating me not to sell her out. She let me know that Jerzy told her about me, and who knows how much he told? Then came her little warning shot across my bow at the end. Trust me, I'm motivated."

"Wow." Seamus crushed out the cigarette. Glanced out the window. Looked back at me. "You know what this means, don't you?"

I'm fired? No sense saying that, so I shook my head.

"This thing is worth *way* more than two-hundred-thousand dollars. We may get our million yet."

My "anything for the team" line to Seamus was a fib, if by "fib" you mean "bare-faced lie." I hadn't slept with Jerzy to lure

him into MVC's stable of power-player wannabes. Nor because
his curly black hair and boyish smile paired perfectly with his
nut-brown face, and with sky blue eyes that came from Heaven-
knows-where. That stuff hadn't hurt, and when he'd picked up
his violin after I mentioned the Creole/Cajun thing and just
tossed off "Jambalaya," grinning like the captain of the football
team at the homecoming dance, I'd decided he'd be something
special even without the money. But I wouldn't have hopped
into bed with him. Wouldn't have cheated on Rafe with him,
which I'd never done before with anyone.

No, I can remember clear as yesterday the first time
my body didn't just say "someone special" about Jerzy but
whoa-Mama-WOW!

It was my second visit to his estate in Maryland. In his oversized living room, prim talk (at least on my side), singing him
the MVC gospel with follow-ups on what we'd talked about
the week before, taking notes on my laptop about questions
and comments he had, all very professional. He'd thrown in a
few suggestive remarks in a slight, charming accent that wasn't
quite German and wasn't quite Slavic, but I'm used to that and
I'd taken it in stride.

Then his Droid had buzzed with a text. He'd given me an apologetic shrug and the screen a quick glance. Suddenly—*Action!*

"My most profuse apologies, but I'm afraid we have to cut
this short."

He'd rushed those words, spattering them at me like grease
popping on a griddle while he'd whipped off his silk Armani
sport coat. Five quick strides to a locked cabinet at chest level in
floor-to-ceiling bookshelves in the far corner of the room. Not
a hint of wasted motion. Key out by the time he'd reached the
cabinet, door unlocked and open in what looked like practiced
movements. Then he'd pulled a shoulder-holster with a muscle-
bound revolver in it out of the cabinet.

Slipped his arms through the holster's straps, pulled the gun
out of the holster, snapped the cylinder out, checked it, snapped
it back into place, re-holstered the weapon—all in about five

seconds. Then he'd pulled the coat back on—and the shoulder-holster hadn't bulged. He had to have had the coat tailored to fit over the holster without showing it, even to someone who knew it was there.

He hadn't looked at me once in the entire process. Then, at the very end, as he moved toward the front door and gestured to me to leave, mouthing apologies and telling me he'd e-mail me about our next meeting, he'd caught my eye and held it. And he'd smiled. I'd read the smile as saying *Well, now you know.*

On the way out the door he'd said, "Nothing to get sideways about. Hundred to one against any drama. The gun is just in case."

"As the Boy Scouts say, 'Be prepared.'"

"A very sensible attitude. But I am not a Boy Scout."

In a way, of course, I'd already known before laying eyes on the weapon. Known he didn't make an honest buck, that he trafficked in a gray, shadowy underworld where "illegal" was a relative term. But I hadn't known it like I knew it at that moment. Jerzy Schroeder wasn't just a crook, more or less. Jerzy Schroeder was a dangerous guy—someone you didn't want to cross.

And that had turned me on. I didn't try to figure out why right then. I had plenty to chew on without bringing Freud into the discussion.

Chapter Six

I waited until Seamus was tied up with a couple of fracking enthusiasts before I closed my office door and used a phone that's none of Seamus' business to drop the Lexus-hustle story on Terry Fielding. Terry isn't a total whore. He's a freelancer who has stuff pretty regularly in the *Times* (the *Washington Times*, not the real one), the *Examiner*, *Rotunda*, the *Daily Boot*, and *Impolitic*. Plays things straight, doesn't betray sources, and what more can you ask?

He sounded studiously unimpressed at the bait, but that was just tradecraft. I knew when he asked me how I'd stumbled over the Lexus-scam morsel that he'd bitten.

"Jerzy let it slip one time when he was trying to impress me. I didn't think much about it at the time. Actually sounded pretty legal. After the murder, not so much. I've done a little checking and, sure enough. Court action last year."

"You wouldn't happen to have the name of the U.S. Attorney leading the case, would you?"

I gave it to him. I didn't include the guy's telephone number. That would have been showing off.

"This is very public-spirited of you."

"I just want the murderer caught—and whoever it is, the police won't catch him if they aren't looking for him."

I got that line out with a straight face. Not that it would have made any difference over the phone, but I have my pride.

"Then why don't you just tell the cops about it yourself?"

"Death-wishes are for Democrats."

"Citizen of the year, that's you, Josie. Is this leak exclusive to me or are you shopping it all over town?"

"Yours and yours alone."

"Scout's honor?"

"Have I ever lied to you?"

"You've lied to me more times than I could count if my cock were an abacus."

I self-censored a crack and continued, "Exclusively yours, Terry—and may my blessed Uncle Darius Zachary Taylor Barry rap my knuckles if I'm lying."

My next call—this one on the cell phone Seamus knows about—went to the lady in gray. I expected voicemail but she picked up on the third ring.

"DeHoic."

"Hi, Josie from MVC. Getting back to you."

"With good news, I hope."

"Mostly. Talked to the boss and we see a way forward here. Very promising. But we don't think we can accomplish your objectives for low six-figures. We're sort of a go-hard-or-go-home outfit. You know, do it right or don't do it at all."

"How much?" The world-weary disgust that dripped from those two syllables could have filled Nietzsche's quota for a month.

"We're thinking a million if you want the best."

"I don't want the best. I want good enough."

Hmm. Set the hook or not? Go with your gut.

"Maybe you and I should talk to the man together. Get all three of us with our legs under the same table, I'm thinking we can find common ground."

"I've just gotten back to New York, I have commitments here on Friday, and I hate flying commercial. That's why I use the Mercedes between the Big Apple and D.C. I couldn't get back down there until the middle of next week."

Two ways to go here. One, suggest that Seamus and I pop up to New York over the weekend. Very accommodating, but it would make us sound really anxious to make a deal. Two, push back a little and see how much of a hurry *she* was in. I opted for two.

"How about next Wednesday afternoon, with a standstill 'till then?"

Thoughtful pause. *This is working!*

"That will do." *YESSS!* "But the standstill has to be bullet-proof. The deliverable is one hundred percent of the file with nothing copied or transferred after this moment."

Gulp!

"Understood."

"Expect me at two p.m. unless you hear differently before then."

I would have said goodbye, but she'd already clicked off.

On my way to the parking ramp that evening—sorry about the carbon footprint, but the D.C. Metro sucks and it's one-point-eight miles between work and home—I got *paparazzied* for the first time in my life. Guy had an actual camera with a lens and everything, not just his cell phone. Called my name, I gave him a startled look, and he triggered one of those motor drives that snaps off, like, eight shots in three seconds.

Hmm. Rafe and I had a plan. Josie in the news wasn't part of it.

Damage Control Strategy, Day 2

(the first Friday after the murder)

Damage Control Strategy, Day 2

(the first Friday after the murder)

Chapter Seven

5:37 a.m.? Really? But it could be Seamus. Or a prospect.

I picked my cell phone up from the nightstand and blearily checked caller ID: Uncle Darius. Groaned. Slipped out of bed and headed for the hall even though I didn't have a stitch on so my impending frank and candid exchange of views with Uncle D wouldn't wake up Rafe. Reminding myself that Darius had taught me a lot over the years, some of it legal, I started speaking slowly and calmly into the phone.

"Unc, you do understand that it's five-thirty in the morning here, don't you?"

"Which means you've been out of bed for an hour, right?"

"No."

"Funny." He was in full drawl—a bad sign. "Every profile I read about one of you Washington power types, it says he gets up at four-thirty."

He had a point. Washington seems perpetually caught up in a personal sleep-deprivation competition. If you're not out of bed and checking e-mails and blogs before five a.m., you're a slacker.

"That's just not the way I roll, Uncle D." I leaned against the wall and raised my right foot to knee level so that I could brace myself with my heel. "And anyway, I'm not looking for a profile."

"You might not be lookin' for it, your serene highness, but that don't mean you ain't gonna find it. Take a glance at *Rotunda*."

With chilly goosebumps on a forced march along my arms, I hustled toward the dining room to fire up my computer.

Remembered that *paparazzo*. I'd checked *Rotunda* and all the
Beltway gossip sites last night, just before going to bed, without
finding a thing. Hated the idea of anyone deciding I was important enough to generate pixels about me in the small hours.

I'd booted up the laptop and was clicking on *Rotunda* when
Rafe whizzed by, heading for the kitchen. He tossed a yummy
terrycloth robe over my shoulders. While I snuggled into it I
found the snippet Uncle D had called about:

> Congratulations to promising starboard money-bun-
> dler Josie Kendall (above, in an unguarded moment)
> on coming through the ambush slaying of shadowy
> one-percenter Jerzy Schroeder without a scratch.
> Well known for blowing smoke up media orifices,
> Josie is keeping uncharacteristically mum about the
> Schroeder deal because (according to her employer,
> Majority Values Coalition), the cops have asked her
> to. No confirmation of that from actual cops, so
> we'll just have to take MVC's word for it. Speaking
> of MVC, it's been panting for years to suck at one of
> the NRA's cash-cow teats. Maybe this is the opening
> it's been waiting for: JOSIE (in medium close-up):
> "If only I'd been packing heat, Jerzy might still be
> alive. I'll never leave home without my Colt again."

"Well," I said after I'd worked my way through it, "they spelled
my name right, and I might put the media-orifices quote on my
resumé."

"Josephine Robideaux Kendall, you're supposed to be a quick
study."

"That's what everyone has always said. You used to tell me
that my mind was like the rapids on the Tangipahoa River: fast
but not deep."

"All right, then, Ms. Quick-Study, what's the most important
word in that snarky little piece of left-wing tripe?"

"Um, uh, hmm. 'Money-bundler'? That's kind of defama-
tory, I guess."

"'Promising.'" He waited for a searing insight to scald my brain. Didn't happen, so he spelled it out for me. "'Promising' is what you call someone who's new to the game. A rookie with a high ceiling."

"Well, I *am* kind of a rookie at activist-group fund-raising. The Congressman deciding not to run for reelection in 'fourteen caught me flat-footed, so I grabbed the MVC thing. Figured I could work my Hill contacts and learn on the job."

"Exactly my point."

"Oh."

"'Cause I'm guessin' you didn't pull Mr. Jerzy Schroeder from the ass of any Congressional staff acquaintance."

"True. I met him at an after-party that the National Association of White Collar Criminal Defense Attorneys threw for a Kennedy Center gala a while back. Just walked up and introduced himself to me. Wasn't even sure who he was, but I remembered what you always told me—'Don't believe everything you say, and don't say everything you believe.' Worked out real well. Until the, you know..."

"Josie, you know as well as I do that you are *too* new at money-bundling—excuse me, development—to have ripe fruit just fall into your lap like that."

Rafe set a steaming mug of freshly nuked dark roast coffee in front of me—just in time to keep me from losing my temper with my condescending relative.

"Now, Uncle D, don't be jumping to conclusions here. You're awful smart, but you haven't been in D.C. in quite a while. Social media has changed things. Networking and relationships happen a lot faster here now."

"'Haven't been in D.C.,' my ass. I was in Washington just three years ago."

"That was for your parole hearing, Uncle D." I sipped coffee.

"Technically my hearing on modifying my conditions of supervised release. For a good long time now, the United States Parole Commission has had about as much to do with parole as the Justice Department has to do with justice."

"Where are you going with this? Are you saying Schroeder was just leading me on—dangling a payday in front of me as bait for an indecent proposal?"

"Nothing of the sort." He managed an indignant snort. "No man who showers regularly and owns a clean suit has to go to that much trouble for horizontal recreation with a smart, pretty girl in Washington. Not as smart and pretty as you, maybe, but close enough if all he has in mind is fun."

"Well, thank you for that."

"I meant it in the kindest possible way."

"So what *are* you driving at, then? What cards was Schroeder hiding?"

"I don't have the faintest idea. That's what troubles me. The purpose of my call is to suggest that after you give that very question some careful thought you let me debrief you so that I can undertake some discreet inquiries."

A chill from my neck rippled right down to my hips. In Louisiana politics the expression "when push comes to shove" isn't a metaphor. Politically active since he was fourteen, Uncle D has done plenty of pushing and plenty of shoving. A Darius Z.T. Barry inquiry is about as discreet as the invasion of Iraq.

"As usual, you are as right as a Pythagorean triangle, Uncle D, and I will do exactly as you suggest." *Up to a point.* "Thank you for sharing your concerns with me."

"You are most welcome, Josephine. You'll always be my favorite niece. I will look forward to hearing from you."

Laying the phone on the table, I stood up so that I could pull the robe around myself properly. Then I took a long hit from the mug.

"Sounded like an interesting conversation," Rafe said.

"Uncle D and Bull Durham cigarettes have two things in common: they come on strong, and neither one has a filter."

Chapter Eight

I sagged back into my chair. Rafe sat down kitty corner from me. He took my left hand in both of his.

"You're cold."

"'Thanks, I needed that' is an unpromising way to start the morning."

Instead of launching into a four-point response to the Uncle D problem, Rafe met my comment with eight seconds of blessed silence. Empathy radiated from his face. When he spoke, his voice couldn't have been gentler.

"How do you feel about that?"

I swam a couple of laps in his dreamy dark eyes. *This guy got up an hour before normal to wrap a robe around me and make me coffee and just BE with me.*

I'd put in about a year on Congressman Temple's staff when I met Rafe. I'd been treating D.C.'s male twenty-somethings as a buffet, sampling this one and that, sometimes intrigued, occasionally impressed, but never blown away.

Rafe had blown me away. One good look and *POW!* His suave urbanity, his easy patter, his sensitivity, his humor, his smarts, his cool sophistication—I'd found out about all that stuff down the road. I'd fallen for him before he'd opened his mouth. It wasn't just his looks. I sensed something about him, some magnetism, some deep-down authenticity. *This guy is real.* I'd been playing Triple-A ball, and I'd just met my first major leaguer.

I'd learned that in his late twenties he'd married a woman he really loved, Leslie Weymouth. They'd planned everything out: start trying for kids in six years or so, when she'd be thirty-two or thirty-three. It didn't happen right away, but she'd gotten pregnant by thirty-four. A boy. Everything about the pregnancy going just fine. She was about four months along when, at dinner with three other couples, she got this startled look on her face, said "What's happening?" and then dropped dead. Basically, her heart exploded. A genetic abnormality, the doctor had said. It could have killed her at any time from the day she was born. She could have died with it at eighty-seven, but instead she died from it at thirty-four. The baby never had a chance.

I think that heart-breaking agony must have deepened Rafe, taken him to a level of humanity that people don't reach too often in D.C., or in Baton Rouge, for that matter. In the eleven years between Leslie's death and the day Rafe and I met, he hadn't gotten serious about any other woman. He got serious about me in a big hurry—and vice versa.

"I feel like a self-involved drama magnet," I told him in response to his question. "This is about you, not me. You're under a criminal investigation, and here I am stewing about some scheme so hypothetical even Uncle Darius couldn't imagine what it might possibly be."

Rafe swung my computer around to scan the *Rotunda* squib. Flicked his head left and right with an appraising look on his face, the way he did when he was thinking *yeah, maybe, I guess, could be.*

"So he thinks you were being played."

"Yep. And if he's right, the game might not be over yet."

"Big if. But I knew Darius before he was a full-fledged grumpy old man, back when he was just a curmudgeon-trainee. I was only a baby reporter for the *Richmond Times*, but even then I could tell that, as politicians go, he was pretty shrewd."

"And as cannons go, he was pretty loose," I said. "Still is."

"Yeah. I remember telling him during an interview that I'd heard that in Louisiana, politics is a contact sport. He said, 'Son, ballroom dancing is a contact sport. In Louisiana, politics is a *collision* sport.' He stole that line from a Michigan State football coach, but he proudly claimed it as his own. Colorful guy."

"More than colorful. After Uncle D did his patriotic duty in Vietnam, he went to work politically in Plaquemines Parish. He was still a Democrat back then, but in Louisiana there were Democrats and then there were *Democrats*. As primary time approached in 1970, according to the story, one of the wrong kind of Democrats took it into his head to inspect the Plaquemines Parish voter registration rolls. When he approached the clerk's office, he found Uncle D and six of his closest friends blocking the door. The fella showed Uncle D a court order. Uncle D showed the fella a forty-five caliber pistol."

"Any shots actually fired?" Rafe asked.

"No, just some fisticuffs. More than eighty percent of the registered voters cast ballots—many of them, remarkably enough, in alphabetical order—and the local dentist took himself a real nice vacation that year."

"Yeah, that pretty much fits his profile. Not sure whether there are too many problems worse than having him try to fix them." *Didn't sugarcoat it. Good.*

We just sat for thirty seconds or so, communing in silence. Didn't know what I wanted to do. Going back to bed made no sense. Couldn't generate much enthusiasm for early breakfast. Obvious strategy for the *Rotunda* squib was to ignore it, so nothing proactive on my near-term agenda.

All of a sudden Rafe jumped up like an overdose of Viagra had just clicked in. Eyes wide, showing his teeth in an open-mouthed grin, animation lighting his face. Looked like Rafe thought I needed a tumble and a cuddle. I figured I should play along because bruising your guy's ego is a lousy way to thank him for robe and coffee.

I'd read him *way* wrong.

"How about a run? We haven't run together in weeks. Not far. Half-hour tops. Get out of here, clear our heads, and pump some endorphins into our flaccid Beltway bloodstreams."

Wow! Rafe had just nailed it.

"You're on!"

I was already out of my chair and on the way to the bedroom. Dressed in five minutes flat. Would've been four, but I noticed Rafe lacing up a pair of blah New Balance court shoes that looked like they'd come from the back of the closet.

"Where are those Nike Air cross-trainers you were so happy about when you paid two hundred dollars for them? That was just, what, a few weeks ago, right?"

"Can't find 'em. May have left them at Capitol Fitness last time I was there." He deftly finished tying his left lace. "Let's go."

We went. Astonishing how exhilarated I suddenly felt. Running at six a.m. is the kind of thing you do when you're nineteen and think having a mid-term coming up is a big deal. Cruising out the front door and heading for the C&O towpath was like scooping all our Beltway hassles into a dog-waste bag and dumping them on a convenient compost heap.

By three minutes into the run we'd gotten our wind and fallen into a comfortable pace that kept us side by side. It was cool going stride for stride like that with my life-mate. Rafe turned his head toward me and asked a question without panting much.

"So what were the next steps on the Schroeder project when he caught the bullet? Were you still at the thirty-thousand-foot level with him, or was an actual buy-in dynamic on the horizon?"

Kinda sad, but I didn't need a translation for that question. Not sure how it happened, but somewhere along the line MBAs started telling political science majors how to talk. Or maybe Rafe was just too much of a gentleman to ask me flat out if Schroeder and I had gotten past finger-fucking (at the professional level).

"I'd say we were right on the verge of a clear path forward. He wanted to take me to a key meeting that very morning and, if it worked out, to head to Denver the first part of next week and meet with the whole brain trust."

"Key meeting with Dierdorf? Here?"

"With the major investor, not Dierdorf. Dierdorf was the target."

"Right. I thought maybe he was thinking of trying to talk Dierdorf out of the game by flexing MVC's fearsome muscle at him. Denver trip on his nickel?"

"Yep."

"Sounds like he was getting serious for sure."

"Yep."

Now I pulled just a little ahead of Rafe. Not by trying to; just happened. I slowed a little to make sure I didn't put too much distance between us. Kinda liked the side-by-side deal.

Funniest thing, the next thought that worked its way into my brain was Sandra Jane Burke, one of my classmates at Carondelet. Hadn't thought about her twice since AP exams. She didn't stay in my thoughts for long, because before we were much more than half a mile into the run Josie the Scold stomped into my brain and launched into an old-fashioned, down-home talking-to.

That's a good man you've got there, Josie Kendall. He's sweet to you and cares about you and fun to be with. You need to be good to him, now. You start takin' a man like that for granted and next thing you know you and your little Creole butt are on the outside lookin' in—and when that happens, won't be no fixin' it by sayin' five Our Fathers and ten Hail Marys.

Not that I took Scoldie's lecture sitting down. I reminded her that ever since Jerzy Schroeder's close encounter with eleven grams of lead had focused the cops on Rafe, I had been dedicating myself body and soul to his problem. Didn't faze her.

You know EXACTLY what I'm talkin' about, young lady, and don't you pretend you don't. Every single mornin' two dozen women in D.C. tell the mirror, 'Why, look, I'm just as sexy as Josie Kendall and twice as smart.' If you can't show your man you appreciate him, one of them for sure will.

Guilt, in other words. Not real familiar with that feeling, and it confused me. In Baton Rouge husbands and wives, generally speaking, don't get all worked up about a dalliance here and there or an occasional little *lagniappe*. You don't go rubbing anyone's nose in it, of course. You don't get surprised in your own bed, or have your picture posted online with a handful of the wrong fanny. As Uncle D would put it, though, "It ain't cheatin' if you don't get caught."

Now, when it comes to this sort of thing, Washington is Baton Rouge with mediocre cooking. I'd figured that out before the end of my first summer there. In this mini-universe of Schedule C appointees, A-listers, senior staff, wannabes, Beltway bandits, lobbyists, and reporters who cover them all, occasional adultery isn't a firing offense. It's just barely a frowning offense.

No one ever spells this out. It's understood. I'd never talked about it with Rafe. I figured it was the kind of thing you just *knew*, like you just *know* anything you say to a reporter is on the record unless you agree ahead of time that it's not. But there was Josie the Scold, and she didn't sound convinced.

"Turn up ahead there?" Rafe's voice, from right behind me.

I nodded. I glimpsed him pulling his left hand away from his right—and I saw the iPhone in the left. Checking our times, I guessed.

On our return leg the run went from good to perfect. I got that runner's high they're always talking about where it feels like there's no strain, scarcely even any effort. Just gliding along feeling forever twenty-one with my muscles stretching and my lungs filling and my heart pumping. Rafe panted up to our front door no more than a second behind me. Checked his iPhone first thing.

"How'd we do?"

"Twenty-eight minutes, for just about three miles."

"So…something north of nine minutes a mile."

"Yeah. I guess we'll be skipping the Olympic Trials again this year."

Grinning, he opened the door and, with exaggerated gallantry, bowed slightly and gestured for me to go in first.

I did. Turned around on the line where the stonework in our entryway stops and our oak flooring starts. I waited until he'd come in and closed the door before I jumped him.

Chapter Nine

I'd call the next two hours just real nice. Showering together and sponging hot, sudsy water all over each other's bodies. Drying off with almost new Prussian blue towels that we'd bought together. Popping him a good one on the fanny, just for luck. Fixing a Cajun omelet—green peppers, onions, sausage, cheese, the whole deal—and sharing it. Mellow, lingering glow kind of stuff.

There was nothing wrong with the sex in between the shower and the omelet, either. I didn't have to fake a thing. There wasn't quite the zing that tasting forbidden fruit with Jerzy had sometimes generated, but Hell's bells, life isn't all espresso and double bourbons. For grown-ups—lucky ones, anyway—it's mostly lattés and smooth merlots and gently subtle Chablis with nuances that a teenager couldn't appreciate.

As I approached the end-game on my half of the omelet, I noticed Rafe idly spinning his phone around on the table. Then I picked up a naughty-eight-year-old look in his eyes. He'll get that sometimes when he's thinking he might have to take a pol to a "gentlemen's club" where the patrons stuff twenties into g-strings, and he's sneaking up on telling me about it (or not).

"I might have set a better pace for you on our run if I hadn't been fussing with this thing," he said.

"You had to keep track of the time, honey." Supportive bride, that's me. "Heaven forbid we wouldn't have quarter-splits on our impulsive fun-run."

"Actually, I wasn't just checking times." He couldn't have sounded more sheepish if he'd been scoping out porn while we were pounding the pavement. "I was following up on a hunch. Turned out to be a good one."

I dropped my fork. Forearms on the table. Full eye contact. "You have my complete and undivided attention, Rafe."

"The National Solar Power Entrepreneurial Conference is meeting next week. In Denver."

"Denver."

"Right. Mile-high city."

"Next week—when Schroeder was talking about getting me there, supposedly to meet with his wind-power hustlers."

"Uh, yeah," Rafe said

"But the odds are a hundred to one that the competing solar power mavens who are *also* going to be there at that very same time will include Sanford Dierdorf—the guy Schroeder and Majority Values Coalition and I were talking about ruining so that Schroeder could glom onto his government subsidy."

"Yep." Rafe sketched a shrug. "Could be a coincidence, of course."

"Sure it could."

I turned a full-bodied scowl away from Rafe. Looked like Uncle D was right for sure—which meant that the clever, quick-thinking Beltway insider profiled on MVC's website had probably been getting herself gamed like a hayseed fresh off the bus from Bug Tussle, Texas. Plus, I still had no idea of exactly what the game was.

Our land-line picked that moment to ring. Rafe answered and immediately put the call on speaker, mouthing *Danica* at me.

"Have you seen *Rotunda* yet?" Seamus asked point-eight seconds after hello.

"Sure have." I infused a nonchalant tone into my answer—and that took some work. "Seems to me we just shrug it off, but I'll be in by nine-fifteen if you think we should work up some kind of a counter-attack."

"Not sure." No trouble imagining what Seamus did during the next ten seconds; when he isn't sure about something, tobacco stocks spike. "Our 'no-further-comment' citadel is under full frontal assault from every keyboard-jockey in town."

"In other words, you've gotten three calls from reporters this morning."

"Two. But it isn't even nine a.m. yet."

The pause that followed was "pregnant" if by "pregnant" you mean "nine months along and fully dilated." I finally spoke up.

"I gave Terry Fielding a tease and promised that my leak was exclusive to him. If we cheat on that he'll cut our balls off. That means we have to keep stonewalling everyone else, no matter what. So…"

"Right. So the only other play I can think of is the helpless-female card."

"Hate it," I said.

"Worked for Hillary in New York and New Hampshire," Rafe said.

"I rest my case."

"It won't be an easy angle for us to work," Seamus said. "But maybe we just have to find a way. I know it makes your skin crawl, Josie, but…"

I cringed. Rolled my eyes. Clenched my fists 'til my nails dug into my palms. Got a grip. Deep breath. Okay. Finally trusted myself to speak.

"It's more important to do it right than to do it fast, SD." I took another breath. "I'll get to the shop as fast as I can so we can talk the options over."

"You said 'options' like there's more than one. I hope you're right."

"So do I."

Just before I could disconnect, Seamus added the perfect coda.

"One other thing to consider on your way in. Do you think there may actually be something to that potential NRA thing *Rotunda* snarked about?"

Chapter Ten

When I got to the office I found the helpless-female issue on the back burner, thanks to Terry Fielding. He'd come through in a big way: the *Times*—the real one: the *New. York. Times.* Just up, posted online about the time I was pulling into the parking ramp, and slated for page eight of tomorrow's hard-copy edition. Already picked up by RCP: RealClearPolitics, the mother-lode aggregator website for political junkies.

Thirteen blessed paragraphs. The headline alone practically had Seamus drooling:

```
INVESTIGATORS LOOK AT
POSSIBLE LUXURY CAR SCAM LINK TO
D.C.-AREA AMBUSH SLAYING
```

Seamus and I skimmed the article itself—me for the first time and him for the third—providing each other with murmured running commentary:

SEAMUS: Big-time property seizures and sealed indictments.

ME: The seizures alone make this a huge deal.

SEAMUS: Yep. The two guys the feds seized the property and money from can't be too happy about it.

ME: Jimmy Matsuyama and Stan Surakawa. Think the feds will flip them?

SEAMUS: They'll have to catch them first. Says later in the article that they've apparently fled the country.

We'd been leaning over Seamus' desk with our eyes glued to his computer screen. Now we both straightened up. Seamus looked over at me.

"You clearly weren't Fielding's only source."

"Yep. Looks like he did some actual reporter stuff."

"Which means that his colleagues will all now be madly chasing the criminal angle too."

"Right." I shrugged. "Which takes the heat off MVC."

"Off MVC," Seamus said, "but not off you. You're a prime source on the criminal stuff. They'll be coming after you—and when the Washington media pack is in full cry, you don't want to be the fox."

Okay, girl, suck it up, now. Curtain going up. No time for stage-fright. I turned to Seamus and met his gaze.

"Seamus, I am twenty-seven years old. Before I'm thirty-five I want to work in the West Wing of the White House. I want to map out talking points for the President while I'm flying on Air Force One for questions we've just found out will be asked as soon as we land. I can't go in front of cameras and choke up and blink back brave little tears because all these big bullies are being mean to me."

"I get that, Josie. But what's the alternative?"

"Tough it out through the weekend. See if the story still has legs on Monday. Odds are it won't."

"What if it does?"

Well that was just a very good question. I didn't have a good answer, so I shrugged and gave a bad one.

"We'll see, I guess. We'll just have to see."

I kind of enjoyed it at first. Calling reporters back, I mean. Got voicemail half the time and just left the can't-comment sound-bite after the beep. When I got into actual conversations, they fell into a pretty standard pattern:

"Now, Jerry [or Tom or Samantha or Caitlin or whatever], you know I can't talk about that while the investigation is going on."

"You talked to someone about it."

"It's funny, but I read Terry's piece this morning and it looked to me like his only sources were public records and a U.S. Attorney in a blue state somewhere. But I guess if you want to know Terry's sources, maybe you should ask him."

"Very funny. Look, Josie, if you wanna stonewall that's up to you, but it's starting to look like you were trying to get into the pockets of a very shady guy, and you're the only one with the other side of that story."

"Why, Jerry [or whoever], I'm surprised at you! That's blaming the victim if I ever heard it. Shame on you. You have a nice day, now."

It got old after awhile, but the scribblers weren't drawing any blood. I got some actual work done in between calls, too. Finished a work-up about a lady in Claremont, California, who has one percent of the stock in two Fortune 500 companies and a burning passion to get the United States back into space and on the way to Mars. Sure oughta be able to do something with that. When I logged off my computer and got ready to start the weekend, I was feeling pretty good.

Then I got home.

Chapter Eleven

I had slipped out of my shoes and taken one good sip from my martini when salt-and-pepper showed up for Act II. The black detective had a bolt-action rifle with him. As soon as the front door had closed behind them he pulled the rifle's bolt up and back, then held it out horizontally, laid across his hands just above waist level, so that Rafe could get a good look at it.

"Is this the weapon you sold several years ago, sir?"

"Do you mind if I take it in my hands?" Rafe smiled. "I mean, you've done the fingerprint thing and all that?"

The detectives looked at each other. Without any nod or other bodily signal that I could see, they apparently reached agreement.

"Go ahead," the black detective said.

Rafe lifted the rifle carefully from the detective's hands. Pointing it diagonally toward the ceiling but without putting the butt on his shoulder, he closed his left eye and looked up the breech with his right. Then he brought the weapon down to chest level and examined the barrel and the bolt as if he were checking the lung X-ray of a forty-year smoker. Gave the trigger and trigger-guard a good look. Worked the bolt twice, snapping it in, then up and back, each time. Now he raised the butt to his shoulder and sighted along the barrel as if he were aiming at a speck in the molding.

While Rafe was going through this, I took a closer look at the two detectives. They must have given their names the first time, and I'm really good with names as a rule, but I guess I was too rattled to absorb them. The black detective had some years and some miles on him. White, not gray, dominated his bristly moustache, and splotches of it dappled his shortish hair as well. A little taller than Rafe, solid build but with a touch of middle-aged spread challenging the lines of his dark gray Men's Wearhouse suit. The white detective was younger but pushing forty even so, about the same height, a little stouter.

The first time I'd seen them I hadn't come away with much more than generic images: black and white, inexpensive suits, basic cop look—like representatives of a sample demographic in a poll I had to analyze. They hadn't really become specific individuals to me until now, with Rafe giving me eighty seconds with nothing to do but look at them and feel their vibe while he messed with the rifle. I suspected that Rafe had picked up all this stuff right away, the first time around. We both have people skills—we pretty much have to—but Rafe's are natural; mine are learned and practiced.

Rafe finally lowered the rifle, shaking his head.

"I can't say I recognize it. It's a Winchester bolt-action and I'd say it's either a three-oh-eight like mine was or maybe a thirty-aught-six, but it doesn't have the feel I remember from the one I owned. That color variation on the barrel tells me that at one time it had mounts for a scope, which I never used. Doesn't prove anything. Just saying. Best guess is no. Does the serial number match up?"

"The serial number has been machined off." The white detective took the rifle from Rafe and gripped it in his left hand, about halfway up the stock. "*Thoroughly* machined off."

"Too bad." Rafe shook his head. "Because, you know, that would answer the question for sure."

"Yeah." The black detective sighed, rolling his eyes.

"Listen," Rafe said, "if you want to talk about this in more detail, how about if we go into the living room? You can get a little more comfortable, and we can maybe find something cold for you to drink. Beer, or ice-water if beer is against regulations."

They jumped at that. Our living room is cozy, reflecting one of Rafe's Beltway axioms: if you want to entertain more than six people, use an embassy. We'd selected Philadelphia blue and Williamsburg green for the room and furnished it in Early American except for a gas fireplace and an upright piano. Salt lingered on the edge of the room, expecting to accompany me to the kitchen when I fetched Dasani over ice. I think I disappointed him when I whipped it up from our cunningly discreet wet bar.

Seated on the front edge of an Ethan Allen fan-back chair, the black detective had retrieved the rifle from his colleague and was showing it to Rafe again.

"We found this a few hours ago. Some schlub driving a stolen car without plates. The rifle was wrapped in a blanket under the backseat. Not a ghost of a print on it, of course."

"Why would the killer conceal the gun in a car and then invite police attention by driving around with no license plates?" The puzzled look that Rafe offered was absolutely priceless. "Especially when he went to all the trouble to take the serial number off to make the rifle untraceable?"

"One theory might be that the guy in the car got set up by the actual killer." The white cop said this, with a scowl suggesting that he was getting a little tired of Rafe's naïve bumpkin routine. "For one thing, we didn't find a scope with the rifle. You mentioned that mark on the barrel that looks like it was made by a scope-mount. Even without that, four hundred fifty yards is a *loooong* way for deadeye marksmanship with just a notch-and-bead sight. Figures there had to be a scope, so where is it?"

"Good point," Rafe said with an approving nod.

The black detective jumped in. "Killer steals a car, replaces its plates with temporary dealer plates, does the murder, wipes the weapon, stows it in the car, drops the car in a strip mall lot or someplace, and ditches the temporary plates. He figures ten to one it gets stolen. Best case the car goes to a chop shop where they find the gun, don't realize it's hot, and sell it to someone who needs a gun real fast—with the buyer becoming suspect number one if the weapon ever turns up. Not-best case, but almost as good, the car thief gets arrested and we pin the rap on him. Either way, case closed."

"Sounds plausible." Rafe bobbed his head sagely—laying it on a little thick, if you ask me. "But you've obviously seen through it."

"Interesting thing about filing a serial number off metal," the white cop said. "If you heat the metal and photograph it with infrared film, the number shows up again. Like magic."

"That'd be great if you could pull that trick off here." Rafe's face glowed with joyful enthusiasm.

"Yeah, it would." Black detective. "'Cause if it turned out it had the same serial number as your rifle that'd be, like, an incredible coincidence."

"I'd be surprised if that happened. The chap I sold it to didn't seem like the shady sort."

"He's seemed like the dead sort for the last couple of years." White detective.

"Not foul play, I hope. It would be cruelly ironic if he were killed by a stray bullet in a drive-by shooting, or something like that."

"Nope, natural causes." Black detective. "Didn't seem to keep much in the way of archives, either. Most off-premise gun dealers don't keep any more than they absolutely have to, even when they're alive and kicking and in business. So we can't verify your sale to him of the rifle you owned."

"Well, I'm really glad you can do the infrared trick, then," Rafe said. "Otherwise there'd be a one-in-ten-thousand or whatever chance that the murder weapon was tied to me."

The detectives exchanged glances. Then the white one sat down on the twin to the black detective's chair and leaned forward.

"Before we turn the rifle over to the lab, we were wondering if you'd remembered anything else that might help us with the investigation." He shifted his eyes toward me. "Either of you."

"We've racked our brains, Detective," Rafe said.

"Drained our memories," I added.

"But if we come up with anything else," Rafe said, "we'll be certain to get it to you as fast as we can."

"Tell me something, Ms. Kendall," the white detective said then. "Did your visits with Mr. Schroeder always end in a walk in the area near that fish pond?"

"Not always. Sometimes. I went out to his farm seven or eight times, different times of the day, depending on his schedule. We probably took that backyard walk two or three of those times."

"What part of the house would you usually meet in?"

"Depended on his mood and the time of day. He often didn't get out of bed until ten in the morning, so once or twice we met in his bedroom with him still in his pajamas and copies of the *Times* and the *Post* strewn all over the bedclothes. He had a Luddite thing about reading newspapers online. Just hated it. Other times we'd meet in what he called the music room, 'cause he played violin and he liked to show off a little. At least once I remember us meeting in his kitchen over mugs of coffee. Plus, he liked to walk while he talked, so we might wander through different rooms or take a stroll outside."

Without missing a beat, without the hint of a segue, the black cop looked a little harder at me than he had up to then, and shot me a question out of left field.

"Did he have any weapons that you knew of?"

Whoa. Did NOT see that one coming. Didn't let it throw me, though.

"At least one. A handgun. Revolver. Not sure of the caliber, except it was bigger than the twenty-five-caliber automatic my Mama keeps around the house, and seemed a little smaller than the military forty-five my uncle showed me from his Vietnam days."

"How did you happen to find out about that one?"

"He showed it to me the second time I came to his farm. Explained later that he liked to go plinking with it sometimes. That's what he called it. 'Plinking.' We went out back on one of my visits and spent about twenty minutes taking potshots at soup cans. He seemed to get a kick out of watching me do it."

"You?"

That question came from the black detective, but I had the feeling that, behind his eyebrows, Rafe was asking himself the same thing. I shrugged.

"Oh, yeah. He asked me to try a couple of pops, and I'm a good sport. Bang-bang-bang."

"How'd you do?"

"Fine. Six shots, six plinks. I'm not world class when it comes to marksmanship, but it doesn't take Annie Oakley to hit a tin can lying twenty feet away."

"Would your office have known what times you were meeting with him?"

"Not precisely. My calendar would say something like, 'JS twelve-three,' meaning that I'd blocked out that time for a meeting with him. So they'd know I'd left the office at noon and expected to be back by three, but they'd have to guess about when we'd actually be together."

The black detective glanced at the white one. The white one glanced back. Then he looked at me again.

"Did you know that Mr. Schroeder had surveillance cameras in every room of his house?"

That was bullshit, so it didn't get the reaction from me that I think he was hoping for.

"No, but it certainly wouldn't surprise me to learn that he had."

Pepper swung his eyes back to Rafe. Salt followed him. When he spoke, the black detective's tone was about two fingers short of apologetic.

"Mr. Kendall, you're being very cooperative. We don't have a warrant, but—"

"You don't need a warrant. Look, I get it. Guy gets killed a few feet away from a beautiful woman, the woman's husband gets a good, long look. We're knee-deep in the twenty-first century and women meet men professionally every day, but 'a kiss is still a kiss,' *et cetera, et cetera*. If I were in your position I'd be doing exactly what you're doing. How can we help?"

The cops exchanged glances. In my mind I whistled in admiration. *Is my guy good or what?*

"We were wondering if we could take a look at your shoes," the black detective said.

"Sure." Rafe pulled off the same New Balance cross-trainers he'd run in that morning and handed them over. "I have two or three other pairs upstairs in my closet. We can go up together and get them, if you want."

"Only two or three?" the white detective said joshingly. "You must be a guy."

"'Brilliant deduction, Holmes.'" Rafe matched the cop's between-us-boys grin.

In his stocking feet he led the white detective upstairs while the black detective compared the soles of the cross-trainers to a printout that looked to me like it had to be next to useless—but what do I know? When Rafe and the white cop returned, they'd left Rafe's dress shoes—a pair of black Allen Edmonds Park Avenues and a pair of oxblood Hickey Freeman slip-ons—back at the bedroom. The only shoes they brought down were a pair of Rockport waffle-stompers that Rafe used for serious hiking. After a hard look at those, they shook their heads.

"Do you own any other shoes?" the white detective asked.

"I may have a pair in my kit-locker at Capitol Fitness. Can't remember, to be honest. I don't get down there as often as I should, and frankly it's starting to show." Rafe patted his almost board-flat gut while he unholstered his phone. "Hate to send you on a wild goose chase, but I guess you can't leave any stone unturned. I'll text Johnny to open it up so you can take a look if you think it's worth the trouble."

The black detective turned back to me. I wouldn't call his eyes hard. Gentle and coaxing, if anything. But I would definitely call them focused.

"Do you know of any other shoes your husband might own, Ms. Kendall?"

"No, I can't say that I do." I grinned—my winsome grin, the one that would make Pollyanna blush—as I gave the answer without hesitation. "I have an uncle who sometimes says if a man doesn't own shoes older than his wife he's not worth month-old crawfish pie, but Rafe isn't that type."

"You're sure about that walk in the garden thing, now that you've had a chance to think about it?" the white detective prompted. "That's not something you and he did every time you went out there?"

"Nope, can't say that it was."

"Thanks," both detectives said at once as they stood up.

They left. They didn't take any of the shoes with them. I retrieved my martini while Rafe mixed a G&T for himself. He sipped. I spoke.

"Well, this sucks."

"Yep."

Chapter Twelve

Rafe and I talked it through while we savored the cocktails and then fixed dinner together. Spinach salad and baked Atlantic cod with lemon sauce—nothing you could screw up just because you had your mind on something else.

"They're hinting at some half-assed theory that you collaborated with the killer." Rafe took more than a sip from his diluted gin. You might almost call it a gulp. "That you arranged to get Schroeder to a particular spot at a particular time so the shooter could ambush him."

"That's what it sounded like to me, all right. But it doesn't make sense."

"It doesn't have to make sense. It just has to scare you."

"Oh."

"They think you know stuff about who the killer is that you aren't telling."

"Well," I sighed, "at least they're not targeting you anymore."

"Oh, no way they've given up on me yet. Ninety times out of a hundred in a murder like this the husband would be the killer, and those odds are too good for them to shrug off."

"But you have an airtight alibi."

"A solid alibi," Rafe said, nodding, "no motive except dirty-minded locker-room insinuations, and they're apparently coming up empty on physical evidence."

"Well, since you didn't do it, of course, it would figure that there'd be no physical evidence."

"A comforting thought. So by now they have to be thinking that maybe someone else shot this guy. They believe you know something, and they're hoping you'll come across if you think that you're a target of the investigation yourself."

"Then why did they question me in front of you? I've binge-watched enough cop shows to know that you question witnesses separately."

"Because they were trying the same psychology on me." Rafe had suddenly gotten kind of intense. "They hope that if I think a cell door might be slamming behind you I'll do some gallant Virginia cavalier thing to save your neck."

I took a couple of seconds and a nice long hit from my glass to process that. Belly drop. Hollow gut. Jelly legs.

Rafe and I both knew what the real threat to me was. There was not much danger of anyone charging me with setting Jerzy up, but that wasn't the point. Think about why Hillary Clinton scrubbed her e-mail server. Inside the Beltway, once someone starts investigating X, what you worry about isn't so much X as Y and Z and all the other stuff they stumble over while they're turning up squat on X. I'd spent six full-time years grabbing for the brass ring on the Washington merry-go-round, including occasional fund-raising for a Congressman and full-time dollar-diving for MVC. In all that time had I committed any felonies? *I had no idea.*

That was the point. You can break the law without realizing it, without meaning to, without wanting to. And even if your heart is as pure as Snow White's, a prosecutor can make it *look like* you've broken the law, or might have, if he really wants to. There is no such thing as raising serious political money without coming into contact with crooks—and that's whether you're raising it for Democrats or Republicans, liberal do-gooders or conservative true believers. Stuff that would never have been a problem becomes a PROBLEM when investigators run across it while they're looking for something else.

This epiphany triggered my standard defense mechanism: flippant denial.

"I have nothing to hide. My life is an open book."

For the third time in our five years together, Rafe got a little macho with me. Okay, a lot macho. He's never hit me. Even the one time I smacked him he hadn't hit me back. I'd stood there waiting for a slap that didn't come. Instead I'd gotten the mother of all hard looks, showing not just anger but disappointment. That had brought tears that no slap would have. But he doesn't have to get physical. He has a low, calm, woman-now-hear-this tone, and he used it.

"Drop the snark right now. The time for snappy patter is over."

Feeling tears sting the corners of my eyes, I waited for the challenge: *WERE YOU CHEATING ON ME WITH THAT SLEAZY HOOD? ANSWER ME, JOSIE! YES OR NO?* But nothing like that came. Rafe went on, still not yelling but with the same vibe. Intensity blazed from those brown eyes.

"Dial it up, Josie. I mean *way* up."

I wasn't looking at any twenty-first century cultivated East Coast metrosexual enlightened male right now—and I knew it. He reached me in one stride, flung my right arm aside to get my drink out of the way, grabbed me under each shoulder and just around my back with two powerful hands and pulled me roughly up against him. The soft Southern accent that he'd lost a long time ago came back to color his voice.

"Listen, Josie. This is now officially about you as well as me. No more business as usual. We are at war." His voice softened, but not all that much. "We're in this together, babe. We're all in. Doubling down. You and me against the world—which puts the odds slightly in our favor."

He squeezed me in a breathless hug that warmed me in a lot of places the martini hadn't. I hugged him back with my left arm as tears slipped from my eyes. *I don't deserve this.* We broke the clinch. I felt like a dewy-eyed prom queen getting her first kiss from the captain of the football team.

"You are so...wonderful."

He grinned like Harry Truman after the news about Dewey.

"I get that a lot."

Damage Control Strategy, Day 3

(the first Saturday after the murder)

Chapter Thirteen

By Saturday morning, around the time we wheeled our grocery carts to the check-out line at Harris Teeter supermarket, I'd concluded that Rafe and I had overthought things a bit Friday night. The cops figured to be looking for an alternative suspect and they for sure thought I might have some dope that would point them in the right direction. We'd gotten that much right. But they couldn't think they'd make me open up about that by actually coming after me for involvement in the plot. That would cause me to stonewall, not sing.

No, the were-you-a-bad-girl insinuations had to be about Rafe. *If your husband really didn't do it then you must know more than you're saying about who did and you'd better come across with it.* The question about video cameras hinted that they suspected my slap-and-tickle with Jerzy, but Lordy me, if every adultery in D.C. produced a homicide the country would've run out of bullets during the nineties. So the police theory about Rafe's motive was *pour le merde,* if you'll excuse my French. Sooner or later the cops would get tired of drilling dry holes and shift their focus completely to another suspect. Once that happened, they'd have no reason to go over my life with a fine-tooth comb.

So skip the gut-flutters, Josie, and keep focused on the damage-control plan. It's working.

We finally started piling food on the conveyor running toward the cashier. We could've gotten to the self-check scanner two aisles over a lot quicker, but Rafe hates that thing. I'm not crazy about it myself. Rafe, though, would cheerfully smash it to smithereens with his bare hands, just for the exercise. I think he'd wait half an hour to check out with a human cashier rather than use one of those robots.

Even without buying anything for dinner tonight (we'd be noshing at an embassy reception) we had quite a load and the bagger the cashier called for took his time getting there, so she had to start sacking up herself. She kept at it even after the bagger arrived because she had to clear our stuff out of her work area before she could ring anything else up anyway. I started loading double-sacks into one of our carts, hoping that Rafe might take the hint and improve the optics a bit. By now, though, Rafe was immersed in *Impolitic* on his phone screen and wasn't giving thought-one to how this scenario might look to people still waiting to check out.

The man-mountain type in a royal blue Izod behind us had already gotten antsy. He scowled at his groceries as they sat there on a stationary belt. About a half-minute after I'd started loading he growled sarcastically at Rafe.

"Are you really incapable of bagging your own groceries?"

After a second or two of surprise Rafe looked up at the guy. If the gent had just said something halfway polite—you know, *Excuse me, sir, but it would be big help if you'd speed things up by doing some of the bagging yourself*—Rafe would have distractedly murmured, "Absolutely right. Wasn't paying attention. Sorry." Instead, though, the guy had come on like an asshole, so I figured he was in for a little Rafe-in-your-face. One look at Rafe's broad smile confirmed that.

"I am in fact quite capable of bagging groceries." Rafe said this in an unhurried, irenic voice, relapsing joyfully again into a Southern accent. "Particularly in these troubled economic times, though, I feel that we should do everything we can to promote employment—and that means not doing for free labor that the management of this store should be paying workers to perform."

Definitely not the kind of soft answer that the Good Book says turneth away wrath. The guy looked confused, like he thought Rafe might actually be serious, but maybe was just mocking him, and he couldn't decide which. Banter apparently wasn't his long suit. It took him five seconds to come up with something, and what he produced wasn't really worth the wait.

"Hey! I work for a living too!"

"I assure you, I had not mistaken you for a day-trader living on his income." Rafe clicked his expression over to earnest. "Once the objective and subjective conditions of proletarian consciousness have converged in your mind, I'm sure you'll grasp the soundness of my position."

Three tense seconds followed. Absolutely delicious. The big guy had two beefy, white-knuckled paws on the handle of his now-empty cart. His purple face clashed badly with that blue pullover. He was pushing the cart as hard as he could. It was going precisely nowhere. Without making a production out of it or getting red-faced or anything, Rafe blocked the cart's front, pressing his thighs and groin against it. I noticed that he had also subtly nudged the outside front wheel so that it pointed toward the next register over. As unobtrusively as possible, I pulled our second cart out of the way to clear an exit route for Rafe.

"You trying to be smart with me?" the guy demanded then.

"That would strike me as a singularly unpromising approach," Rafe said, still smiling and jovial. "By the way, don't forget to put that toilet paper on the bottom of your cart on the belt so that the cashier can ring it up."

"What?"

In the half-second the guy spent looking down at the empty rack underneath his cart, Rafe nimbly put some daylight between himself and the front of the cart. When the guy looked up he petulantly shoved the cart forward. Instead of slamming against Rafe, though, the cart dinged the working side of the other register station. By the time the guy had pulled his cart back and straightened out the wheels, Rafe had made it out of the narrow lane between the two registers and was helping me load the last two bags into our second cart. Glancing back at the guy, Rafe sketched a casual salute with his left hand.

"See you at the revolution!" he called cheerfully.

I managed to keep it together until we'd made it to the parking lot and were closing in on Rafe's Ford Escape. Then I lost it. Started with a giggle, tried to control it, failed. Threw back my head and just laughed. Bent over the cart handle and laughed. Felt tears streaming from my eyes.

The whole thing was perfect. Absolutely perfect. Manmountain had started it, Rafe had finished it, brains over brawn, no blood—oh, Lord, forgive me, but I loved every second of it.

We started loading groceries into the hatch. Rafe was flat out glowing.

"You do realize that if that oaf had been exercising his constitutional right to keep and bear arms, you'd probably be dead now, right?"

"True." Rafe grinned "And the last two minutes of my life would have been the best."

Chapter Fourteen

Now, the only reason I brought up that male head-butting episode is that it saved my life.

A thought began percolating below the surface on our way home. It reached full brew not quite six hours later. I was getting ready for that embassy reception. Freshly showered and made up in the understated way Mama taught me, I was fussing with an earring when I happened to glance at the open door to Rafe's closet. Noticed those New Balance cross-trainers that he'd worn during our run. And did *not* see the fancy Nike Air things that, as I now remembered, I'd watched him fork over two hundred dollars in cash for two or three weeks ago.

Cash. Who uses cash for a purchase that big? Someone who doesn't want it showing up on a credit card bill? *Boing!* Almost dropped the earring. A lot of things came together.

What if he did it? What if Rafe DID kill Jerzy? Unbidden, memories of Jerzy flooded my brain: Jerzy flashing his infectious smile, ladling out his smooth conman banter, hot-dogging it like a self-aware schoolboy with his violin. I imagined Rafe, the man I loved, the man whose children I hoped to bear, coldly gunning him down. All this time I'd taken Rafe's innocence for granted. I'd pooh-poohed the jealous-husband motive because of how civilized we are here about matters of the heart, and related body parts. Did I need to re-think that?

I thought about the self-scanning check-out thing. Uncle D used to quote my great-grandfather's Sunday dinner rants against supermarkets. "Sure the A&P can charge rock bottom prices. They have a store full of free clerks working for them!" Great-gramps had grown up in a world where a clerk behind a counter in a general store fetched your order item by item as you called it out. He'd liked that world just fine. The world replacing it as he grew older, though—not so much.

Rafe was a generation older than I was. Maybe self-scanning check-out was his A&P—a symbol of the ground shifting under his feet. The arrival of a lifestyle that he didn't like as much as the way of life he'd grown up with. A lifestyle where no one knew what honor was anymore and people were rude in supermarkets and "white male" was a dirty word.

Maybe Rafe had a lot more old school in him than I'd thought. Maybe he'd brought more Richmond with him to Washington than I'd imagined. That cast a new light on the motive thing. The American South outside Louisiana is a whole different country, brother. "Unwritten law" they call it down there. You blow away a man who's fussing with your woman—that's flat out justifiable homicide for nine juries out of ten.

I started looking at things with different eyes. Sure, Rafe could easily have sold a rifle a few years ago without my knowing the first thing about it. But hunting rifles are almost like hound dogs for sons of Dixie. When one of them parts with a firearm that he's used to kill large mammals, he can mope nostalgically about it for days. I sure didn't remember anything like that.

He'd told the cops his eyesight had gotten too weak for big game hunting. But he'd spotted the two cops behind their windshield from eighty feet away and nailed their descriptions.

Rafe could have used someone else's computer to find a conveniently dead gun dealer without documenting his curiosity on his own search-history. He could have forged a receipt. He could have paid cash for a pair of shoes for the express purpose of wearing them to an ambush site, and then dumped them somewhere just in case he'd left any footprints or picked up any incriminating twigs or soil. He's a cocky rascal, for sure. If he'd planned the whole thing carefully, he wouldn't have had any trouble pulling off the super-cooperative witness act with the police.

He could have bought a beaten up old car for a few hundred in cash, using a false name. Could have stashed the rifle in it after the murder and left the car to be stolen, just like the cops said. Could certainly have filed the serial number off the gun. Maybe he hadn't known about the infra-red trick, or maybe the cops were just bluffing about that.

But what about the air-tight alibi? He'd spent the day with Theo McAbbott, and his phone documented that.

No, no, it didn't, did it? The phone proved that the phone was in McAbbott's house—not that Rafe was. The cops had obviously talked to McAbbott, though, and they hadn't shown up with an arrest warrant after the chat. So McAbbott must have backed up Rafe's story. That meant that either Rafe's story was true, or McAbbott was an accessory to first-degree murder. You can die in jail for that one.

Why would McAbbott risk life without parole for Rafe? McAbbott would have known from his FBI years how huge the risk of getting caught was and how many ways even a perfect plan could go wrong. Rafe couldn't have gotten McAbbott on the Supreme Court. Couldn't have gotten him on the Board of Tea Inspectors, for that matter. Sure, a man's gotta do what a man's gotta do, but as far as I knew they hadn't shared a foxhole or backed each other up in a knife-fight or done any macho bonding stuff like that. They had a professional relationship. Rafe got McAbbott's crime stories published and made a modest commission for his trouble. Nothing that would make you dive on a grenade for someone.

That left money. Everyone has a price—and in politics it's usually a lot lower than most people might think. I've been in committee hearing rooms in Baton Rouge where you could buy anyone at the table for fifty bucks and a ham sandwich. Add three zeroes and you could say the same thing about Washington.

A vote on a pork-barrel project is one thing, though, and a one-way ticket to the slammer is something else. How much would Rafe have had to come across with to get McAbbott's soul in his hip pocket? Hundred-thousand? No way. It was a nice piece of change, but wouldn't change your life. A million? I suppose. Maybe.

But how could Rafe possibly have gotten McAbbott a million dollars? Rafe and I aren't really rich, although I guess a lot of people would say we are. Net worth of a little over two million— most of it Rafe's under the pre-nup. But none of that wealth is just sitting around in cash in a basement strongbox. Mostly the house and stocks and bonds. Could Rafe have converted them into that kind of cash without leaving a paper trail wider than the road to Hell, as Uncle D would say? I sure didn't see how. Besides, I would have noticed—wouldn't I?

Nope, offhand, I just couldn't see any way to get there from here. That air-tight alibi was starting to look like your basic stonewall. Rafe couldn't have killed Jerzy unless he had some way of getting to McAbbott that I just flat couldn't think of.

I suddenly felt a whole lot better. Looked like I wasn't married to a cold-blooded murderer after all.

Chapter Fifteen

Some things never get old. Embassy receptions aren't one of them. They started getting old for me around the third or fourth one I attended. Just another day at the office now. Sip, nosh, meet, greet, mingle, network, repeat.

This Saturday night's reception happened to be at the Indian Embassy, so we had curry instead of escargot or talapas on the steam tables. Otherwise it was pretty much the same as it would have been anywhere else. Embassy receptions these days usually have co-sponsors that are trying to promote commercial interests in the host country. Tonight: the Telecommunications Equipment Manufacturers' Association. The evening's tone generally comes more from the co-sponsor than from the flag on the roof.

Rafe wore a white dinner jacket, black slacks and cummerbund, white shirt with onyx studs, and black bowtie. In Rafeworld, that's what men wear to semi-formal affairs in summer. Period. The tuxedos and regular business suits vastly outnumbering dinner jackets in the reception room suggested that Rafeworld is a fairly small place. I guess that's one of the things I like about it.

We got our drinks together—G&T for him and seltzer with a lime twist in a Manhattan glass for me. Figured I'd better pace myself in case I had to do some serious drinking later on. Then we split up. Rafe spotted a couple of cable news producers in a loose group at the other end of the room and headed for them like a torpedo homing in on an aircraft carrier. Didn't spot such obvious prey for myself right away, so I decided to circulate a bit and see what turned up.

Nothing much at first. I greeted people right and left and blitzed through little snatches of casual conversation during my steady sashay toward the room's center. As I clicked on each entry in the digital Rolodex in my head, though—House Democrat; Foreign Service Officer; Senate Judiciary Committee senior staff; print media; National Security Council junior staff; digital media; Commerce Department lawyer; cable/broadcast media— I didn't see anyone I had any real use for at the moment. No SEC or Federal Elections Commission. No one with a hundred-million dollars burning a hole in his pocket who was passionate about Chinese unfair trade practices or excessive limitations on mining federally owned land.

Then, out of the corner of my eye, standing not far from a sculpture of a glossy green elephant, I spotted Robin Vauss, chatting up a guy showing me the rear of his head and the back of a tux. I wouldn't call Robin super-pretty, but no guy would kick her out of bed for eating crackers either, as we say in Baton Rouge.

Robin has a full-bodied mane of chestnut hair framing a sculpted face suggesting a central European countess on some remote branch of her family tree. Not sure what color her eyes are because she switches daily among contact lenses in at least three tints—violet, green, and chocolate brown. Without sleeping with her—and I'm not planning on *that*—I guess I'll never know the color nature actually gave her. Smallish frame, maybe a smidge shorter than I am, nice breasts, not-bad legs, and between cigarettes and forty-minute Elliptical workouts she keeps her hips and tummy from getting too prominent.

Robin can be just the nicest semi-insider in Washington between the time she gets up and somewhere around four-thirty in the afternoon. From then until she's had her third cosmopolitan, though, her default facial expression goes to something between pout and scowl, and her mean-girls streak starts showing. She has some kind of on-again/off-again thing with a Hoover Building suit named Vince Ashland. Not a special agent, a "process manager" or something like that.

The guy with his back to me looked vaguely familiar but didn't look like Ashland. Pickings tonight were slim, though, so I headed discreetly for the elephant. I figured that even a ten percent chance of talking to someone who gets a check from the Federal Bureau of Investigation every two weeks justified a tentative foray in that direction. You never can tell when one of those boys will let something slip.

I edged closer. Nope, not Ashland. With a little start, in fact, I realized the guy she was talking to was M. Anthony York, my lawyer. Not all that much of a coincidence, really. Insider-Washington is a pretty small place—not quite Hooterville with monuments, but not Metropolis either.

As hunks go, Tony is a Hell of an attorney. He can shift into smooth-mode when he wants to, though, and the first words I overheard him say were right there.

"What's the most interesting thing you've done this week?"

"Had sex with an ex-president," Robin answered. "How about you?"

"Sang 'Bye Bye Miss American Pie' all the way through by heart."

"You win."

Off again, apparently. Oh well.

I started to glide politely away. I pretended not to notice when Tony tried to catch my eye. Robin, however, didn't pretend not to notice. The comment I heard from her just before I slipped out of earshot was, "Steady, boy. The last guy who flirted with her got his cerebellum perforated." *Hmm...* That glass in Robin's hand must be only her second cosmo.

"Pretty snarky crack," I heard someone say from my right and just behind me. Recognized the voice: Lizzie Nygren. Staff reporter for the *Washington Inquisitor*. Regular panelist on a cable news/chat show with ratings just above local access. Got a ton of Facebook shares early in the race for the Republican presidential nomination when someone asked whether Scott

Walker not having a college degree should make a difference and she answered, "Jimmy Carter had one and Harry Truman didn't. Next question."

As I turned a big smile in Nygren's direction I tried to think of one other thing I'd heard about her. Instead of dredging up that last datum, unfortunately, my mental Rolodex kept cycling through an endless loop like that maddening blue circle I sometimes get on my computer screen.

"Still playing it close to the vest on Jerzy Schroeder's murder?" she asked.

"I'm just as sorry as I can be, Lizzie, but I'm afraid I can't talk about that."

"Actually, you already have talked about it—just not to me."

"I believe we've already had this conversation."

I could see her gearing up for a world-weary sigh and a let's-quit-playing-games pitch. As she started to deliver it, the last entry in my Lizzie Nygren data-set finally popped up. Air Force Academy. She'd left in the middle of her second year. Her permanent cover story was that she'd gotten tired of putting up with a culture of sexual harassment. Persistent rumors, though, said that she'd been expelled for cheating on her final exam in electrical engineering.

"Look, Josie, the suspicion hanging over your husband isn't going away—as Robin's little rim-shot ought to tell you. If you really want to spin it off the stage with an alternative theory, you need someone with more horsepower than Terry Fielding has, to pump out the copy."

"I just want the police to catch the murderer—and the sooner the better. If I can help them by keeping my mouth shut, that's what I'm gonna have to do."

"Yeah, yeah, yeah." World-weary sigh, right on cue, accompanied by an eye-roll. "Look, Josie, you're not playing this very smart."

"I very much appreciate your candor, Lizzie, which I am sure is well meant. I realized long ago that the words 'Nobel Prize' will not appear in the first sentence of my obituary. I did, however, manage to graduate from an accredited American university after passing all my examinations without any improper assistance. So despite my limitations I guess I'll just soldier on as best I can."

For just a second I thought she was going to splatter my face with bourbon and sweet. Lord, that would have been wonderful. Every reporter in town would have had the full story on it within an hour. Nygren didn't just think about it, either; her right hand actually twitched. But she dialed the impulse back just in time, did a one-eighty, and stalked off.

Well, the hits just keep on coming, don't they? Deep breath, squared my shoulders, kept going. Damage-control operation still functioning, but Nygren had a point. If I'd had to bet on how this would end I'd go with *not soon* and *not pretty*.

I finally managed to track down Kent Ezekiel, a Republican Congressman from the southern part of Florida. I planted a seed about the good old days of the Apollo program returning; get America back into space; on to Mars—that kind of thing. His eyes lit up. Any self-respecting Congressman can make his eyes light up if all you do is give him your recipe for grilled cheese sandwiches, but I decided to take it as a good sign anyway.

Time to find Rafe and see how he was doing. About two hundred seventy degrees through my systematic sweep of the room, I spotted him forty feet away, talking to Major Fitz. "Major" in this case isn't a rank. It's the first name Fitz's mom and dad blessed him with. He is African-American. He is gay. Still has a little hitch in his step from an IED in Iraq, back when he was Lance Corporal Major Fitz. Taller than Rafe, slender, and with hair made for the cover of *Ebony* or *Esquire*—take your pick.

Major has a twice-weekly column in *Impolitic*. He covers and comments on Washington politics as if that were a white-collar crime beat—not much of a stretch, if you think about it. Nicest guy in the world unless you've used your office to steer a defense contract to a company that has you lined up for a lucrative speaking engagement in Hawaii.

I hesitated. Even from a good distance I could tell that Rafe and Major were having more than a casual chat. Shrugged and started working my way toward them. Rafe could wave me off if he thought I'd be in the way.

It became moot point. Out of nowhere Tony intercepted me. Nudged me toward a quieter area, near a statue of a multi-armed Hindu goddess.

"Why, Tony, I thought you'd be between the sheets with Robin by now."

"If by having sex I could justify bills like the one you're getting for tonight, I'd be in the movies. We have to talk."

Chapter Sixteen

Tony ushered me out to a balcony that ran the entire width of the building, populated only by a handful of smokers. Even at foreign embassies, where D.C.'s cigarette police don't have jurisdiction, public smoking in Washington is about as fashionable these days as men's white dress shoes. I turned toward Tony.

"You're on. Go."

"Had a chat with Rafe's lawyer today. Cops have *nada*. Alibi holding up, no holes in Rafe's story, no physical evidence, no witnesses who can put him at the scene or going to it or coming from it."

"Good news."

"Up to a point. Their only hope is to shake the alibi by proving that Rafe somehow paid McAbbott off. So they want to have forensic auditors crawl through every account, stock, bond, and dollar you and Rafe have."

"Well, that sucks."

"Yep. On the bright side, it's their last bullet. So to speak. On the not-so-bright side, will something like that be a problem for you?"

I swallowed. Hard. Rafe and I play it pretty straight, but there's no such thing as an audit that doesn't turn up something a little smelly here or there.

"If we tell them to get a warrant, they'll think they're finally barking up the right tree, won't they?"

"Yep."

"Okay." Deep breath. "If Rafe can handle it, I can. I'll go along with his call."

"Not so fast. Say the audit comes out empty. Rafe will be off the hook, but then they'll need another suspect—and you're the only lead they have to one. You didn't even like being a sideshow. Now you might become the main attraction."

I took a breath—a shallow one this time, and a little labored. The only possible answer was the one Rafe had given me when the shoe was on the other foot.

"If Rafe says yes to the audit, then I say yes." I sipped seltzer and *really* wished it were gin. "But this audit-stuff comes from Rafe's lawyer. If you're going to bill me for schmoozing with Robin Vauss, I hope you learned something from her."

"Oh, I learned something from her all right."

"Spill."

"The local cops aren't flying solo on Schroeder's murder. The FBI has invited itself to the party—and its theory is the partner-in-crime angle that Terry Fielding is peddling for you."

Which meant that Fielding had an FBI source. Hmm...

"You wormed that out of Robin—or did it just slip out because a couple of cosmopolitans loosened her tongue?"

"Neither. She blurted it out to me, and not by accident. Tracked me down and dumped it on me two minutes after striking up a conversation."

"So, a calculated and deliberate leak."

"Yep."

"She told that to you, presumably at her boyfriend's request, knowing that you'd tell it to me." I finished my drink. "Why?"

"Because the Feds are hoping you'll give me a copy of MVC's Schroeder file so that I can get it to them. Unless I miss my guess, they're also dreaming that maybe you'll tell them some juicy stuff that isn't in the file. They're betting that you'll want to help them nail a criminal confederate as Schroeder's killer because that would definitively clear Rafe."

I pondered that. The FBI wouldn't waste time on a local murder unless it implicated a federal investigation that was already under way. An investigation involving Jerzy, for example, as subject or key witness. I had zero interest in auditioning for key witness—especially as understudy to a corpse. That's why I'd come down with that sudden case of lock-jaw the first time the cops asked me who might have killed Jerzy. On the other hand, having the killer *thinking* I could finger him could get me dead just as fast as actually doing it—and if the FBI thought I could finger him, the killer probably did too.

Wow. This was more complicated than a three-candidate election with no primary. I looked up at Tony.

"What's your recommendation?"

"Depends on what's in the file."

Tony favored me with a steady, penetrating gaze. *I'm the only human being on the planet that you absolutely cannot lie to.* He didn't have to spell out the question: *Does that file have anything in it that could make you thirty-seven months late for your next appointment?* Simple truth: I flat didn't know for sure.

"Think it over," Tony said then. "Let's talk about it on Monday."

In other words, "After you've looked at the file."

Chapter Seventeen

Next stop, Rafe. I spotted him without any trouble as soon as I came back in. He and Fitz hadn't moved much, and with the crowd starting to thin it took me less than a minute to work my way over to them. When I got close enough I could tell that Rafe was doing a genial *o-tempora-o-mores* riff.

"Less than three months ago I got a call from this kid." He bobbed his head earnestly at Fitz. "Twenty-two years old. *Twenty-two*. He has his whole career already mapped out. Four years on the staff of either the Senate Judiciary Committee or the House Foreign Affairs Committee. *Maybe* six years, but no more than that. Couple of articles along the way, then a book: *Watching Sausage Being Made*. Already has the title. No contents, but the title is a killer. He figures the book and the contacts he will have been busy making along the way will make him a standard go-to guy whenever CNN or NPR needs a comment on something in his field. Couple of years of that, and he takes a sabbatical for a stint on the White House staff. He'll serve a president from either party. Not picky. After he's done his West Wing time, he figures he returns to civilian life as a male Rachel Maddow, with his own show on a major cable news channel."

I couldn't help smiling. I could have put half a dozen names on the character Rafe was describing. Fitz was laughing out loud.

"I hope you told him that he should get a blond wig and breast implants and go on Fox News as a legal analyst."

"I would have," Rafe grinned, "if I'd thought of it."

"Not like the old days," Fitz said. "And you and I aren't even that old."

"I *know*. Used to be, people took a job in Washington 'cause they wanted to get paid for doing the same thing that got them A's on term papers in high school and college. Now they come because they take a look at their skill set and say: Doctor? I suck at chemistry. Lawyer? Those drones work too hard. Wall Street? I could end up broke or in prison. Regular business? Ugh, *dad* and *mom* did that. No, best way to maximize my lifetime earnings is to stick my snout in the public trough and then leverage the media game."

I sidled into Rafe's field of vision. The instant he spotted me he reached out and pulled me giggling to his side. As he hugged me I made a quick but expert appraisal: *Not drunk. Not close. Good.*

"Good talk, buddy," Fitz said, sketching a see-ya salute.

"Oh, don't mind Josie," Rafe said. "She just dropped by to make sure I don't turn into the Church Lady."

"Gotta move along." Fitz shook his head, smiling. "Keep it real."

"I didn't spoil a pitch, did I?" I got a repentant pout ready in case the answer was yes.

"Nope. Major and I were just playing Those Were the Good Old Days. What's up?"

I told him about Tony's little bombshells.

"So we spun Terry Fielding into an actual, honest-to-God *story* without realizing it?" Rafe asked. "Man, when you're good, you're good."

"And when you're lucky, you're lucky. But it looks like I have to examine every page of that bloody file, even though I agreed to a standstill with DeHoic."

"I'd say you do." Rafe nodded emphatically. "You can tell her that you had to make sure there wasn't anything on there that could get you an obstruction of justice charge if it somehow disappears after she gets her hands on it."

"Right. If she actually has the computer examined she'll know that I accessed the file, and she could tell if I forwarded anything in it to some other computer. Would she also be able to tell if I printed anything out?"

"You have to assume yes," Rafe said. "So don't print anything out."

"Right. I'll just eyeball it—first thing Monday morning."

Rafe gave me that look that Southern boys sometimes lapse into before they remember their manners: *I can't believe that EVEN A WOMAN would say anything that fucking stupid.*

"First thing Monday, my ass. You need to be looking at that stuff tonight."

He was right. He was absolutely right. I *hate* when that happens.

Chapter Eighteen

So that's how I came to be at my desk after ten o'clock on a Saturday night, going screen by screen through MVC's pitch-file for Jerzy Schroeder. Really studying every page this time, instead of just looking for a juicy nugget. Sweating, because the A/C goes off at eight p.m. and I didn't know how to turn it back on. Also swearing a bit at the sheer tedium of this exercise. It wasn't as tedious as doing three-to-five, though, so I slogged on. Had to be something in here that DeHoic didn't want to turn up if a flatfoot appeared with a search warrant. And if that something, or anything else in these pixels, might put my butt in a sling, I had to know about it before some beady-eyed disciple of J. Edgar Hoover did.

Rafe had wanted to come with me, but a thirty-second talk-through pegged that idea as a non-starter. It wouldn't do to have Rafe signing it at the security desk of MVC's building, much less showing up on tape from the surveillance cameras, on the night when digital records would show I'd taken a look at Jerzy's file.

Pushing midnight, I'd reviewed more than three hundred pages of the pitch-file without seeing anything important that I didn't already know. I couldn't get complacent, though. I sighed. Scrolled. Impatiently rubbed away a rill of sweat coursing down the back of my neck. Cut loose with a couple of unladylike ejaculations. Scrolled. Sighed—*bingo!*

Color photograph, showing up quite nicely on the high-res desktop monitor that MVC provided to me. Night shot. Front and center, Sanford Dierdorf—the guy MVC wanted to help Schroeder run out of business and maybe into the slammer. Standing in front of one of those Gulfstream jets that'll set you back eight figures. Smiling. He wore mustard-colored hunting pants. His shirt was Black Watch plaid—again, standard issue hunting garb for rich guys. On his right hip he had a holster with one of those flaps that goes over the handle of the gun it's holding. Growing up I'd known plenty of hunters who took a sidearm with them when they went into the woods for a weekend of Bambicide.

Dierdorf stood next to a woman who bent her head slightly forward as she lit a cigarette. The lighter's flame left no doubt. DeHoic—except that for once the gray lady hadn't dressed in gray. So either Abercrombie & Fitch doesn't sell Outdoor Wear in gray, or DeHoic was trying for incognito. To DeHoic's right stood two gentlemen in dark business suits. Also smiling. With Japanese features.

Okay, nerds, do your stuff. I brought the cursor over the head of the one nearer to DeHoic. The nerds came through. A little white bubble with letters in it appeared over the guy, as if he were saying something in the Sunday comics. Jimmy Matsuyama. Same trick with his buddy. Stan Surakawa.

I hesitated. Printing the page might cost MVC several hun-dred-thousand dollars, get me fired and maybe get me killed. But what if I just clicked the Screenshot icon? Would that make a record? I shook my head. Too big a risk.

Screenshot. Wait a minute. Maybe I couldn't make a screen-shot, but I could sure take a shot of the screen. Whipped out my iPhone. Sort of like a selfie, except taking a picture of something else. *Click!* Checked the image on the phone's screen. Uh, no. Pretty much sucked. Just my luck, there's never a professional grade Nikon single-lens reflex digital camera lying around when I could really use one. *Shit.* I was starting to get a headache. I needed a tablet.

Tablet. *No, Josie, you precious idiot, you don't need a tablet, you need a Tablet®.* I fished my iPad Mini out of my purse. I'd never used its camera feature, but it couldn't be all that hard. Fussed with it a bit. It was pretty intuitive, as it turned out. Frame. Focus. *Click!* Check. Yep. Not a candidate for the National Gallery, but I could make out the faces and read the bubble words clearly enough.

Okay. Another forty-five minutes of scrolling to go, minimum, but I'd found nothing criminal so far and at least now I knew I'd have something to show for my efforts. Something pretty provocative, in fact. I sat down to get back to work.

The hallway lights and the overhead lights in my office went off. It happened automatically every sixty minutes. An energy-saver. I got up to truck down the hall and flip the manual override switch—something I'd done twice tonight already. I'd kicked my shoes off more than two hours ago, and I didn't bother to put them back on for this jaunt.

Two steps into the hallway, I heard a distinctive *thunk* from the suite's lobby area. That sound could only mean one thing, and it wasn't good.

Chapter Nineteen

I'd heard the *thunk* a thousand times. An electronic lock holds the big, glass door at the suite's main entrance closed. That *thunk* is the sound it makes when someone unlocks it by flashing a keycard at a sensor tastefully embedded in the mahogany frame on the door's right side. Someone like me or like Seamus—except that I was already here and the pope will be going through her second divorce before Seamus pops by for office hours around midnight on a Saturday.

I crept close enough to the doorway between the hall and the lobby to see the lobby door area. Pitch black. Which it shouldn't have been. There should have been a pale semi-circle of light just outside the doors that stays on all the time. I'd worked enough late nights to know that. Couldn't really see anything in the dark, but a change in the depth of the blackness, combined with the barest whisper of crepe sole on faux marble, told me that someone was pushing the door open and coming in. Time to channel my inner coward.

The intruder would have to go about thirty feet to get to the hallway. I'd have to go about twice that far to get to Seamus' office—I sure as Hell wasn't going back to *my* office, and his was the next closest. Advantage burglar, but at least I knew exactly where I was going and the burglar would have to feel his way.

I breathed a quick prayer to St. Monica and started moving. Slow and steady, backwards the first few yards, then I turned tail.

Bare feet on pile carpet, I could move almost silently if I just kept it to one measured pace after the other instead of thunder-footing it like a hippo in heat. I figured that the risk of being heard if I started hurrying was a lot higher than the risk of being seen, even once the burglar entered the hallway himself. Or herself. Tension rippled through my shoulders and closed my throat. The bad guy had to have made it into the hallway by now—but Seamus' door loomed just ahead on the left.

No percentage in looking back, so I didn't. Stopped. Held my breath. Waited for a sharp challenge or the sound of running feet, which would mean he'd spotted me and I was basically toast. Nothing. I slipped into Seamus' office, budging his door the bare twenty centimeters I absolutely had to in order to get in.

Okay. Give the burglar maybe ten seconds to get to work gutting my computer—because why else would he be here?—and then discreetly dial nine-one-one. Got it made, right?

Wrong. Remember Uncle D's crack comparing my mind to whitewater that runs fast but not deep? Well, right about now it clicked up to Grade Four rapids.

Within seconds the burglar entering my office would see that my computer was on. He'd spot my shoes and my purse. So he'd know I was still here. Maybe then he'd just grab the computer and high-tail it. At least as likely, though, he'd start looking for me. So I definitely *do not* start nattering with a nine-one-one dispatcher, because he'd hear me and know right where to go.

If he looked for me, where would he look? Ladies' room qualified as the most logical place to find me, so maybe he'd go there first. No guarantee of that, though, and anyway, then what? When he came up empty on the loo he'd start looking other places and sooner or later he'd get to Seamus' office—probably sooner. The women's restroom was outside the suite, around two corners from the elevator bank. If I could just be sure he'd gone there, I could haul ass out of the suite and down four flights to the security desk before the intruder even knew I was on the run.

How could I possibly know that, though? I'd been listening as hard as a five-year-old trying to hear sleigh bells on Christmas

Eve, and I hadn't picked up a sound. My whole restroom strategy would depend on pure guesswork.

Then I heard something—and guesswork dropped right out of the equation.

"I know you're in here." Menacing male voice, calm but firm, projecting but not yelling. "I need you to come here. Nothing to be afraid of. I'm not going to hurt you. I just need to keep an eye on you while I do my job."

Dear Lord, I wanted to believe that. It'd make everything so easy. If I fell for a line like that, though, my sainted papa would kick my ass when I met him in Heaven (or wherever)—and I would flat-out have it coming. I reflexively stepped backward, almost lost my balance, and had to put my left hand on Seamus' desk to steady myself. Stifled some colorful Cajun expletives. After a good ten seconds, I heard the voice again.

"If I have to come looking for you, I *will* find you—and when I find you I *will* hurt you. Considerably." A trace of anger stained the voice, which now rose a bit. "You'll be taking your meals through a straw for weeks. I know what I'm doing and I have night-vision goggles. You don't have a chance. Just come out and we'll do this without any bruises."

My knees turned to noodles. Gut churned. Felt like puking. So tempting. *Don't do it, Josie.* Maybe Seamus had a gun. Yeah, sure. Seamus? You kidding? I groped his desktop, trying to find the edge so that I could work my way down to the drawers. I felt a smooth, glossy tube and knew at once what it was—the closest thing to a firearm Seamus was likely to have: one of his six cheap cigarette lighters.

"All right," the voice said. "You asked for it."

Lighter. Picked it up. Grabbed a handful of paper from the credenza behind his desk. Didn't know what it was, didn't care. Flicked the lighter and held its brave little flame to the edge of the paper. Figured that if I could set the paper on fire, I could hold it up to the smoke detector and, if St. Monica wasn't busy with anything else, trigger an alarm that would spook the guy. *Come on!* I mean, you'd think paper would go up just like that, but *nooo*. I could smell smoke and hear crackle and feel heat—damn, could I feel heat—but it didn't strike me as the kind of conflagration likely to motivate a smoke detector.

Well, it's just gonna have to do, that's all. The guy had apparently started with the two rooms on this hallway closest to the lobby: a storage closet and an area with a high-speed color printer and a couple of photocopiers. He thought I was within earshot, so he must have decided I was inside the suite rather than in the ladies' room. He'd just search systematically, making sure he stayed between wherever I was and the lobby. Wouldn't take him long to rule out those first two rooms. Seamus' office would be his next stop.

I raised the smoldering bundle of paper toward the ceiling, in what I vaguely remembered as the general area of the smoke detector. Stood there like an imitation of the Statue of Liberty in a middle-school pageant. Nothing to do but wait and hope, and I didn't figure to have long to do either one. Couldn't see or hear a thing, but I sensed him outside the door. My gut churned. Heart raced.

I heard Seamus' door slam open. The burning papers in my hand now cast just enough light for me to see the dark outline of a black-clad figure, no more than ten feet away.

"Okay, bitch, I gave you fair warning!"

I screamed. Faintly saw the figure leaping toward me, and not a damn thing I could do about it.

Suddenly my sheaf of paper exploded in bright, pulsing, yellow and blue flame that flared toward the ceiling and scorched the Hell out of my hand in the process. Dropped the burning pages—just in time to hear the smoke alarm start howling like a Sigma-Tau pledge on Hell Night.

I braced myself for a body-slam that would knock me into the middle of next week. It didn't happen—and I couldn't believe what did. The guy stopped in his tracks. Raised his hands to his head like he'd suddenly gotten a migraine on steroids. Bent over the way you do when you take a real good gut-punch. Ripped thick goggles off his head, letting them thump dully on Seamus' singeing carpet.

WTF? I had no idea saints could do that! I hadn't been to Mass since I'd visited Mama last Easter, but it looked like I'd better drop by this Sunday for sure. I mean, *damn.* Short term, anyway, it seemed to me that things couldn't get much better.

Then they did. Automatic ceiling sprinklers came on and started soaking me and the intruder to the skin. I was probably a lot happier about it than he was.

No reason to tarry. Skirting around him, I darted for the door. He grabbed at my legs. Seemed like his heart wasn't in it, but he managed to catch my left ankle with a lucky forearm swipe. I pitched headlong, ate some damp carpet, and started scrambling on my hands and knees. I'd covered about half the remaining distance to the door when he decided to come after me, even though he apparently still couldn't see anything and didn't have much idea where I was. His left foot cracked my ribs and his right buried itself in my fanny as he tripped over me and went flying through the air. I wasn't sure which hurt worse, but I figured neither one hurt anything like as much as the smack he took on the noggin when he collided with the door jamb.

I clambered to my feet, hitched the lower half of my dress up to public indecency level, and flat-out ran over him: kidney, head, floor—then into the hallway. Skipped and hopped a bit, almost lost my balance, banged a shoulder against the hallway's far wall, but managed to keep my feet and sprint for the suite's lobby.

The lobby was still dark except for a flashlight beam big enough and bright enough to stare down a semi-tractor trailer on a two-lane highway. *Accomplice?* Didn't have any better ideas so I stopped cold. A nanosecond later a steely hand gripped my left bicep. At close quarters, in the back-glow from the flashlight, I recognized LaDasha Wallace, a rent-a-cop from the security desk downstairs. Didn't know her, except for a vague recollection that she was a Marine veteran, but I'd seen the nameplate in front of her when I signed in a few hours ago. She must have recognized me, too, because she dispensed with a lot of the preliminary palaver.

"What in *Hell* is goin' on?"

"Burglar. Back there. Not sure if he's armed."

"Well, if he is he won't be for long. Stay *right* here. Don't you *move*."

Handcuffs in her left hand and mega-light in her right, Wallace charged down the hallway like she was hitting the beach at Inchon. The intruder had apparently recovered enough to give her an argument when she started to cuff him. Bad idea—no such thing as an ex-Marine. I didn't see what happened, because instead of staying where I was I snuck back into my office. Near as I could reconstruct things from the raw hamburger where the intruder's face used to be, the blood streaming from his broken nose, and the limp he walked with when the real cops led him off, though, Wallace vigorously defended herself, got his hands cuffed behind his back, then defended herself some more. Except this time kind of a preemptive defense—sort of like the second Gulf War.

I did not pass my time idly while Wallace lent herself to these constructive pursuits. By the time she'd finished with him and D.C. Metropolitan Police officers had shown up, I had accomplished three things: closed out of the Schroeder file on my computer; logged off and turned the computer off; and gotten my scared-and-helpless female look on for the benefit of the constabulary.

Damage Control Strategy, Day 4

(the first Sunday after the murder)

Chapter Twenty

I made it to five p.m. Sunday Mass at St. Matthews in northwest D.C.—the very last one for that weekend. I guess I could have skipped it. The young black police officer who interviewed me told me that the thug acting like he'd just been Tasered was due to night-vision goggles rather than divine intervention. Seems that if you're running around in the dark with those things and a sudden bright light flashes right in front of you, it's like having a strobe light go off in your face, except worse. Even so, to be on the safe side, I snuck into St. Matt's to tell Monica I appreciated what she'd done, just in case she'd done something.

The reason I almost didn't make it was that Sunday turned into a real busy day. Let me re-phrase that. Sunday was a bitch. I finally got home with Rafe around two a.m. Woke up after less than six hours of sleep to coffee and toasted bagels, courtesy of my sainted spouse. I'd just scalded my throat with the first gulp when Seamus rang our doorbell. That's what I said. He didn't call, he actually drove over and *rang our doorbell* at a quarter after eight on Sunday morning.

When your boss does that, you can't really beg off, can you? Rafe found a cup and a seat at the kitchen table for him. Seamus sat down, looking like he was wearing clothes he'd slept in. He hadn't shaved, and any hair-combing he'd managed was on the perfunctory side. I thought his first question might be something along the lines of, "Are you okay?" Wrong.

"Has the asset been compromised?"

"I take it I am not the 'asset' you're referring to. 'Cause that would be an ungentlemanly question if I were."

He started to say something vulgar. Then he realized where he was sitting and glanced at Rafe standing about five feet from him. Instead of saying anything at all, he just looked exasperated. Cue Josie with a slightly less smart-ass answer.

"The thug came after me before he could do anything with the Jerzy file. The sprinkler went off in your office, but not mine. The police didn't take either of the computers, mine or yours, or copy anything. When they asked me what I thought the burglar was after, I told them I didn't know. So they don't yet have any particular reason to want to see…the asset."

"'Yet' is right." Seamus looked a tad dyspeptic. "They'll have plenty of reasons once they put two and two together—which might be fifteen minutes from now."

"Or might be never." I offered him half a bagel, and he shook his head. "Point is, at least as of right now, no one outside MVC has laid eyes on that file."

"So we'll say when DeHoic calls. But she'll assume the burglar came after the file, and she'll think it's a funny coincidence that you just happened to be there when he did."

I shrugged. Once I found out that the FBI had jumped into the case, I had to get a look at the file. Period. The burglar probably found out about the federal involvement even before I did, and late Saturday was the first chance he had to go in. I explained to Seamus about the FBI leak and told him the cover story Rafe and I had worked out to justify my own file review. He went from dyspeptic to sour—a slight improvement.

"Do you really think it's smart for us tell DeHoic about the FBI's involvement?" he asked.

"Well, if she already knows, she'll think we're hiding something if we *don't* tell her. And if she doesn't already know, telling her will raise the price."

"You're right. We tell her."

"'We' as in you, or 'we' as in me?"

"You," he said decisively. "I have to get into the office and see what I can salvage. I'll bet it's a royal mess."

"That would be yes." I gave him a cheerful nod on his way out the door.

Chapter Twenty-one

DeHoic had the decency to wait until after nine o'clock before she called. Nine-oh-three, to be exact—well after the story first showed up on the *Washington Post* website. I usually answer my phone "Josie Kendall," with a cheerful little chirp in my tone, but I barely got the first syllable out before DeHoic repeated Seamus' question.

"Has the asset been compromised?"

"Nope."

"What did he get?"

"Nothing."

Three seconds of silence. I imagined DeHoic wondering whether she should believe a word I said. Based on her next question, she came up with a solid maybe.

"So the Jerzy file is still pristine? No copies, print-outs, or views since we spoke last week?"

"No copies or print-outs. I went through it last night."

"You *WHAT?*"

"Looked through the file."

"That wasn't the deal, goddammit! Why did you do THAT?"

"Because I found out Saturday night that the FBI is sniffing around that file, without having the gumption yet to come right out and actually ask for it."

"FBI." Her voice had suddenly grown calm and quiet, as if she'd just dropped a fast-acting 'lude.

"Right. So I had to make sure there wasn't anything in it that would obstruct a criminal investigation by disappearing. Only one woman in Washington can get away with destroying electronic evidence, and her name ain't Josie Kendall."

"Okay, you looked at it. Did you find a deal-stopper?"

"No. Every scrap of information I saw was either from a public record or from some file the FBI already has access to on its own. Can't see a reason in the world why we couldn't turn the file over to you for the useful purposes you have in mind."

Relieved sigh from DeHoic—the barest minimum thing you could do with your breath and call it a sigh. She had another question all set for me.

"What record did you make of what you saw?"

"None."

"Not a single note, then?"

"Not a scrap." My nose was growing, but I didn't mind as long as it was just metaphorical.

Long pause. Funny, I felt that I could almost hear her thinking, like an echo-chamber voice from inside her head on a TV show. *Change our meeting to Monday? No! That would look like panic and jack the price up.* Not sure, of course, but I'd bet that's awful close to her actual thoughts.

"All right," she finally said. "We'll proceed with the audit and the meeting as scheduled. Expect my techies first thing Wednesday morning."

"Got it."

Chapter Twenty-two

We had a nice respite after that, time to get through the *Post* and the *Times* while flipping among the Sunday morning chat-shows before Tony the Lawyer called not long after 11:30. Before handing me the phone Rafe said, "Sure, Tony, let me see if she's available," so that I'd know who was calling.

"Tony," I began, "if you ask me whether the asset has been compromised, you're fired."

"From a strictly legal standpoint, it might be better for you if it had been."

"Well, from a strictly jacking-up-my-year-end-bonus standpoint it wouldn't be, so I'll take my chances. Anyway, moot point."

"Do you think you'll have an answer for me tomorrow on whether I can dangle anything in front of the Feds?"

"I have an answer for you right now. 'Yes.'" I described the picture, and explained that nothing in the file reflected badly on me. "But you can't dangle it until Thursday morning."

"Shit."

"For what I'm paying you, Tony, you really ought to put the rough language in Latin. Or French, at least."

"*Merde.*" Tony paused while I chuckled appreciatively. "What's happening between now and Thursday morning?"

"We're trying to talk someone into stepping into Jerzy's shoes on the project. Go/no-go by close of business Wednesday."

"And this person won't have any objection to the FBI getting a look at that picture?"

"As long as she doesn't know she won't."

"Okay. Please keep me posted. And can you send me a copy of that picture?"

"Sure. Thursday morning."

Chapter Twenty-three

That took us into the lunch hour. I was ignoring all the calls from reporters, of course. Six, by my count. I was a little hurt that there weren't more. Guess I wasn't as important as I thought I was. Anyway, Rafe and I were scratching out a statement that we'd mass-release around ten p.m. No sense in jousting with the ink-slingers before we did the release.

Then, just after I'd swallowed the last mouthful of Boar's Head ham and Wisconsin cheese with lettuce on whole wheat bread—that's about half of Rafe's culinary specialties, the other half being world-class coffee—the caller ID flashing when the phone rang showed Uncle D's number. I had half a mind to just let it go to voicemail, but an Uncle-D call is like a trip to the principal's office: best to just get it over with.

"Hi, Uncle D. How are things going?"

"Well, I haven't heard from you, for one thing. About what we discussed."

"I'm real sorry about that, but I've been kinda busy."

"So I've just read. Sounds to me, Josephine Kendall, like you are in way over your head. Bushwhacking a gangster is one thing, but burglarizing a man's private office—that is serious business. And I'm betting you are no closer to knowing why that low-life pulled you into whatever his game was than you were the last time we talked."

"I actually have made some progress on that front, but I have to be discreet about it."

"Discreet?" His voice rose. "DISCREET? Josie, it has been a long time since I turned you over my knee, but so help me—"

"In point of fact, Uncle D, you never turned me over your knee. Mama wouldn't let you. And since I'm now twenty-seven years old and we're blood kin, that idea is sneaking up on creepy."

"Figure of speech, darlin'." He used the laugh he does when he's in full retreat. "Point is, if you won't fill me in and help me to help you the easy way, I'm gonna have to start making some inquiries on my own."

"*Please* don't do that." Now *I* was in full retreat. "You are the very best uncle a girl could hope for, but things changed a lot during your little sabbatical. Folks in Washington aren't as mentally tough as they were in your day. They get their feelings hurt a lot more easily. You have a way of coming on that can really rub some people the wrong way nowadays."

"Now where did you hear *that*, may I ask? Emily Blount, wasn't it? Two little headlines, and both of them in Yankee newspapers. Hell, Josie, she didn't lose that election because of me. She lost 'cause she's all tease and no tit. Simple as that."

I sighed. Red-alert warnings were lighting up the inside of my head like the Tokyo Ginza during a geisha special. Had to do something, and buying some time was the only thing I could think of.

"Okay, Uncle D, now just calm down. You're my most important weapon, and I can't go firing it half-cocked or shooting from the hip with it. I need to use your special expertise at precisely the right moment. So you lie low for a while, and I faithfully promise that I will call you next Saturday afternoon with a complete update, and we'll have a little consultation then."

"You wouldn't be stalling now, would you, Josie?"

"You trained me better than that, Uncle D. You know full well that when I say I'm going to do something, I do it." *Except when I don't.*

"Well, that's a fact, I guess. But I'm not an idiot, despite what you and Emily Blount might think. I'm not gonna sit on my hands for a week while who knows what roof collapses on you. I'll hold my fire until Tuesday."

"The way things are going, Unc, I feel like Tuesday is two hours from now. Can we make it Thursday?"

"Tuesday. And try not to get yourself killed or in handcuffs between now and then."

"All right, then. I guess."

I hung up, absolutely exhausted. Drained. I looked up at Rafe—what he calls my "sad puppy" look. He was scratching away on a legal pad at the statement we'd been drafting.

"Problem?" he asked.

"Well, you might say that. Uncle D isn't gonna be happy until he pulls some stunt that gets my name on the front page of the *Post*. Above the fold. And I don't have the first idea what to do about it."

"Up to you, Josie-belle. If it was me, though—excuse me, if it were I—I'd give him a job to do. Something that will keep him busy in a locale that the average Washington reporter couldn't find on a map in three tries."

"What in the *world* could I come up with for him to do that far from Washington?"

"That might take some thinking." Rafe smiled wryly at me. "But as your former boss Congressman Temple used to say, 'If it were easy, a Democrat could do it.'"

Chapter Twenty-four

Rafe's suggestion actually helped. Really did. Gave me something constructive to do instead of just stewing. Between wracking my brain over busywork for Uncle D and flyspecking our draft statement, I ate up almost three hours. Started to mellow out a bit.

That lasted until a little after three-thirty, when our landline rang. Caller ID said "Wireless Caller" with a number I didn't recognize, so it figured to be another reporter and I ignored it. Something funny about the voice when it went into voicemail, though. Labored breathing, outside background noise, and words oddly spaced, as if the speaker were talking on the phone while also doing something a lot more physically demanding.

"Josie, this is...Amanda...Amanda Schnabel. Not a... reporter. We...knew each...other back in...the day. If you... can't...pick up, don't...call me...back. Repeat....*Don't* call me back. Put my ass on...toast...if you do. I'll...leave a...time when...I'll call you...again. Say...tonight—"

I picked up.

"Amanda! Of course I remember you! We met when you were on the staff of the House Subcommittee on Issuing Subpoenas to People Named Clinton, didn't we?"

"Right....Uh...Government Affairs....Yes."

"You're not in labor or having an intimate recreational experience, are you, Amanda?"

"No...I'm running. No one...will suspect I'm...using a phone...while I'm...actually running....Uh, gonna stop now."

"Thank God." I looked at the phone like it had just grown horns and started dripping blood. "What in the name of crawfish pie is going on, girl?"

"I'm with the House Executive Branch Operations Committee now. Staff are subject to a permanent anti-leak inquisition. Anytime you make a phone call from the committee offices, you assume that someone has their eye on you."

"Why didn't you just call from home?"

"On duty. All hands on deck since the story broke this morning. 'EMERGENCY! EMERGENCY! THIS IS NO DRILL!' Committee chair is a fitness freak, though, so going for a run is a way to get outside for a few minutes."

"When you said 'the story,' you didn't mean that silly breaking-and-entering at MVC, did you?"

"That's exactly what I meant. You know Saris, right?"

"Yes, of course. Congressman Adler Saris, committee chair."

"Okay. Well, he's not just salivating; he's frothing at the mouth. As soon as he read that story he talked himself into believing that we have a Democratic Watergate on our hands. You know, Democratic Party operative breaking into a Republican think-tank to get political intelligence."

"Oh no." I put the heel of my hand to my left temple, because I could already feel the headache coming on. "Oh, no no no no no no no. Oh dear Lord, *please* not that."

"'Fraid so, Josie. Unless I miss my guess you'll get your first tickle from committee counsel sometime tomorrow. You can say you have no idea what was going on. You can say that all you want to. But he's not going to let it go with that. If you don't have red meat for him and he feels like he's not getting to the bottom of this, subpoenas could be flying like confetti by the end of the week. Just wanted to give you a head's-up. For old time's sake."

"I really appreciate this, Amanda." By now I was talking on automatic pilot while I tried to get my reeling mind to focus— focus on *something, anything.* "I'll do my level best to be prepared.

And I won't forget how you came through for me on this. You didn't have to do it."

"Okay. Now I have to run back to work. Literally."

Chapter Twenty-five

Believe me, it was one thoroughly shaken Josie Kendall who started getting spruced up around four-fifteen for Mass at St. Matt's. A Congressional committee investigation isn't like a criminal investigation by detectives or FBI agents. A criminal investigation eventually ends. Charges are filed or the case is closed. Once a member of Congress gets his (or her) teeth into something, though, it just goes on and on until every last second of cable news time and every last donation from true believers has been milked out of it. Years and years. Benghazi, IRS/Lois Lerner, Iran/Contra, Tailhook, Army/McCarthy, all the way back to Thaddeus Stevens auditing Mary Todd Lincoln's household accounts during the War Between the States. Forget the headache; I was getting sick to my stomach. Literally.

I held it together for Rafe's sake. He was about to have beady-eyed forensic accountants crawling up his net worth, and he sure didn't need his wife turning into a basket case on him on top of that. I was working myself up to telling him about St. Matt's—I felt a little sheepish about the Mass thing—when he came up from behind and wrapped his arms around me.

"I get it," he whispered into my ear. "I honestly do. At this moment all you can see for yourself between now and meno-pause is lawyers and subpoenas and eight-hour prep sessions for committee hearings."

I nodded, without trusting myself to speak. *I will NOT start blubbering on this man.*

"You have to be strong with everyone else," he murmured. "But you don't have to be strong with me."

Well *that* did it. I wheeled around, buried my head in a chest that still smelled of Dial soap, and bawled my eyes out. Just cried and cried for more than a minute while Rafe silently held me, arms enlaced around my back and pressing me against his body.

Okay. Got it out of my system. Catharsis so complete I should spell it with a kappa, the way the Greeks did when they invented it. Felt tons better. Moving back one step, I looked up at Rafe's face. I didn't deliberately make my expression adorable; couldn't help it; just happened.

"Honey, would it be okay if I went to five o'clock Mass—or do you have plans?"

"How about if I go with you?"

Chapter Twenty-six

My little chat with St. Monica went well, as far as I could tell, even though it was a bit one-sided. Rafe and I had a nice bistro-style meal on the way home. I discovered that I'd worked up a very healthy appetite—always a good sign. Thought of an assignment for Uncle D. So from the end of Amanda's call to the moment we walked back in the door around seven-thirty, my emotional attitude had done your basic one-eighty.

Then Terry Fielding called. As the designated media-whore, he, unlike other reporters, got the privilege of talking to me.

"Deep background, right, Terry?" Figured we'd better get that straight right from the git-go. "'Person familiar with the investigation,' right?"

"Yeah, sure." He sounded impatient, as if my little nicety amounted to fussing with seating arrangements at an execution. "Listen, Josie, important question: have the cops asked you about Jerzy having a handgun?"

"Sure have. I told them he had a revolver he used for plinking around the farm."

"Well, he also had an automatic, and it wasn't designed for casual pot-shots. They found it in a holster hooked to the back of his belt, under his sport coat, when they examined his body. Beretta nine-millimeter. Major piece of hardware."

"Well, I'm not the type of gun enthusiast who can identify makes and models by sight. I can see your point, though. That is definitely not the weapon I saw him with. No idea he owned anything like that."

"Not clear he 'owned' it, Josie, 'cause here's the thing. That Beretta had been purchased over a year ago—by Sanford Dierdorf."

"Whoa!" My head started to spin a bit. I mean, *WTF?* "Jerzy stole Dierdorf's pistol? How? Why? I don't get it."

"I don't get it either, Josie. No one gets it. But Jerzy getting dead while he's four feet from you is one thing. Getting dead while he's four feet from you and armed with a pistol stolen from an obvious suspect adds a whole new level to this thing."

"Yes, I can see where that is an interesting development."

"'Interesting development' doesn't come close. This thing is shaping up as a four-alarm cluster-fuck."

"Four-alarm cluster-fuck." Kind of a colorful phrase, isn't it? I made a mental note of it, in case the occasion to drop it into a conversation with a Sunbelt billionaire might present itself somewhere down the road. Meanwhile, though, I kept thinking. Thought hard and fast. In the damage-control strategy Rafe and I had worked out, Terry was in charge of spinning Rafe off center-stage. At the same time, though, I was in charge of sweating shekels out of Ann DeHoic—who wouldn't want the world to know about a picture showing her with Dierdorf. Whose gun someone had stolen and given to DeHoic's ex-husband. Who happened to be carrying it when he passed away. I'd put that picture on hold until Thursday for my own lawyer, but reporters just don't have lawyerly patience. They don't have any patience at all.

In other words, the two objectives were now in conflict. No, they weren't 'in conflict.' They were slugging it out in a fight to the death, trying to kill each other with their bare hands. Telling Terry about the picture was telling the world. Eight-to-three that would scare DeHoic and her money away from MVC.

In other words, couldn't be simpler: Rafe or my career? *Which one do you choose, Josie?*

"Terry, I need to tell you about a picture."

Damage Control Strategy, Day 5

(the first Monday after the murder)

Damage Control Strategy,
Day 5

(the first Monday after the murder)

Chapter Twenty-seven

Monday better than Sunday, but we're talking about the world limbo championship of low bars there.

Got to work by eight—the Josie equivalent of the crack of dawn—because I wanted to make sure Seamus saw me at my desk when he strolled in. Called Tony the lawyer and told him I'd be zapping the picture to him ASAP and he could forget about the Thursday embargo and get it to his FBI contact pronto. I knew I'd get zero credit for disclosing it if the FBI didn't get it from me until after Terry Fielding mentioned it in a follow-up story—and Terry's next story could appear as early as this afternoon.

Next on my list: Uncle Darius. I had taken three deep breaths and had my index finger hovering over his speed-dial button when an e-mail from Seamus hit my screen. The e-mail had a link. It would have taken priority over the Uncle D call even if it hadn't. Clicked the e-mail open.

"Happy Valentine's Day." S

WTF? Clicked on the link. A piece posted ten minutes ago in *Impolitic* popped up:

```
         IT'S NOT A GAME, OKAY?
         Opinion by Major Fitz

   Assassination-style murder of a rich guy
   is a big story, and we'd all like a piece
   of it. Totally get that. Terry Fielding has
```

gotten himself a couple of three sources—
God bless him; that's what reporters are
supposed to do. He's running with the story
while the rest of us play catch-up. Very
frustrating. Get that too. And we've all
heard D.C. insiders from the President and
Attorney General on down solemnly invoke
an ongoing investigation as a pretext for
stonewalling the press when the real reason
for their laryngitis is a standard-issue
damage-control strategy.

But this isn't about partisan abuse by the
IRS or channeling procurement contracts to
political chums or erasing e-mails sent on
official business. It isn't about any of the
usual Washington BS. It's about a murder. A
homicide. A human being shot down in cold
blood by either a professional killer or
someone doing a damn good imitation of one.
The killer needs to get caught, the crime
needs to get solved, and that needs to happen
without any witnesses getting killed along
the way. This is the one political story in
a thousand where the ongoing investigation
dodge actually has a patina of legitimacy
about it.

Most of us only know of one civilian
source with potentially useful information.
A number of reporters have been hassling
her, blowing off police concerns about her
talking out of school. There's a difference
between due diligence and stalking, and a
non-trivial part of the D.C. Fourth Estate
has crossed that line.

It's time to knock it off. Past time, in
fact. This isn't the usual Beltway game.
This isn't a game at all. This is real life
and deadly serious. So go after the story,
sure. But let's get up off our lazy butts
and develop our own sources, the way Terry
Fielding has, instead of hounding someone
who's already a victim and could become a
bigger one.

◇◇◇

Wow. Whoa. I mean, *damn*. Seamus nailed it: Fitz had written me the sweetest valentine I'd ever gotten. Not only would the Lizzie Nygrens of the world be ducking for cover, but Congressman Adler R. Saris would think twice about getting too aggressive with the comic-opera burglary investigation he was ginning up.

There was not a doubt in my mind about where this came from. This had to be what Rafe was pitching to Fitz when I saw them in earnest conversation at that Indian Embassy reception Saturday night. It's one thing for a girl to be married to a saint; I was married to a *talented* saint with a skill set and a contact list that could make him seem damn near omnipotent. I had Rafe on my side. What could a couple of gangsters, a puny Congressman, a brace of cops, and the FBI do against me?

Giddy stuff, for sure—suddenly I couldn't *wait* to get home. Unfortunately, a steel-reinforced load of gray, concrete, *you-fucked-up-girl* guilt competed with the soaring, romantic high. I'd cheated on Rafe because I'd given in to a thrill sparked by a bad boy with a gun, a soul-stirring shiver of danger. Sandra Jane Burke would have said I was hardwired for it. A conversation a dozen years in the past in Sandy Jane's bedroom came back to me.

"Francoeur," Sandy Jane had said. "You'll go to the junior prom with him. Nappy Lejeune thinks you're all that and a mess of grits and he'd crawl over broken glass for you, but Nappy is on the chess team at SAG, and Francoeur is an outside line-backer"—'SAG' being Saint Aloysius Gonzaga Prep.

"Nappy is first board on the chess team, and Johnny Fran-coeur is second-string on the football team," I'd snapped back, in full pissed off adolescent mode.

"Makes no difference. Females are hardwired to prefer ectomorphs as mates. We don't choose breeding partners based on whether they'll go to PTA meetings; we pick them based on whether they can kill woolly mammoths and protect us from saber-toothed tigers and serial rape."

"Right. And Adam and Eve were playing with dinosaurs in the Garden of Eden before they ate the apple."

"I'm talking Darwin, not Billy Graham. Nappy laughs at your jokes and loves talking current events with you and thinks it's really cool that you want a career in politics. But Francoeur has a letter on *his* sweater because he runs into people and they're on the ground after he does. When he quits fooling around and actually picks up the phone and asks you to be his date, you'll say yes."

Reverse psychology—a Sandy Jane specialty. She thought I should go with Nappy and she was trying to make me pick him out of sheer cussedness, just to show I wasn't a puppet of Natural Selection. It worked, too. But she almost blew it three seconds later. Sitting there cross-legged on her bed, back resting against the wall, Marlboro Light dangling from the right corner of her lips, she threw in what she must have thought would be the clincher.

"Francoeur dated Cheryl Dannault last summer. I saw her once wearing sunglasses on a cloudy day."

That produced the belly-drop Sandy Jane was going for—and a real zing along with it. Risk. Danger. I don't mean I wanted a black eye, any more than you want lung cancer when you smoke your first cigarette, or a fractured skull when you bungee-jump. But the thrill, the idea of facing the *possibility* and going ahead anyway—that had reached me. Thinking about it now, I finally understood why Sandy Jane had popped into my head during my run with Rafe.

I ended up going to the junior prom with Nappy. Sandy Jane came with Francoeur. I should've seen that one coming right down Broadway, but I didn't. She had the grace to smile sheepishly when she saw me, shrug an apology and say, "Hardwired." So we stayed friends. I dated Nappy the rest of my way through Carondelet and into college—right up until he entered the seminary. That seminary thing made him the second man I'd loved who suddenly wasn't there for me anymore. Maybe that's when, somewhere inside me, I started wondering what I'd missed.

Chapter Twenty-eight

No time to bother Freud about it now, though. Had to call Uncle D. He answered on the first ring, with a question.

"You know what day it is, darlin'?"

"Um, Monday?"

"It's the last day of my period of supervised release over the glorified speeding ticket that piss-ant Assistant United States Attorney in northern Virginia nailed me with. As of one minute after midnight tonight, I am officially free of all constraints imposed as conditions of my release from prison. Among other things, that means I will be able to be in legal contact with convicted felons. For the last three years I have been restricted to contact with felons who haven't been convicted yet."

I would not personally put influence-peddling in the same class as going, say, fifteen miles over the speed limit. At least not when it involves an attaché case full of hundred-dollar bills—Uncle D was always a traditionalist. Especially when it turned out Uncle D hadn't had any influence to peddle. But I had heard my dear uncle's rant about how an Assistant United States Attorney, whose own mother wouldn't recognize him in the shower, had more tyrannical power than the NSA and CIA put together. Several times. Didn't want to hear it again. So I did not demur. Wouldn't have mattered even if I had. Without waiting for any comment from me, Uncle Darius went right on.

"In other words, I will wake up tomorrow morning strapped, locked, loaded, and game-ready. Just drop the leash, get out of the way, and let me go."

"Now, Unc, I definitely don't want you doing anything remotely felonious. I don't know what the adjective for 'misdemeanor' is, but I don't want you doing that, either."

"I know you don't, Josephine. Your Mama raised you better than that."

"What I have in mind is getting a little background information on this solar power thing that Jerzy Schroeder was trying to cut out of the federal subsidy game when he passed away."

"That's the Sanford Dierdorf hustle, right?"

"The very one. Now there's this big solar power conference in Denver starting on Wednesday. I wonder if maybe you could get yourself out there and just sort of mingle, soak up the gossip, have a drink now and then with folks who look like they're in a chatty mood. Then this weekend I could debrief you and we could talk about what to do next."

Something like ten seconds of silence followed. Even three silent seconds in a conversation involving Uncle Darius is highly unusual. Ten seconds was completely unprecedented. I didn't have a chance to think about it, though, because Seamus put his head in my doorway. He pointed his left thumb and little finger at his ear and mouth respectively, then pulled his hand away and thrust it toward the floor. *As soon as you hang up.* Then he pointed his right index finger at me, swiveled his hand, and pointed it down the hall. *Come to my office.* I nodded to show I understood what he wanted. By the time Seamus disappeared, Uncle D had found his voice.

"I will surely be delighted to do this, Josephine but, uh, I am er, a little, uh, *embarrassed*—"

"Oh, I'm sorry, Unc. I should have said this up front. I would not *dream* of you being out of pocket when I'm the one asking you to do me a favor. I'll arrange your flight and hotel on my American Express and e-mail you the details. And if you need some walking-around money too, you just let me know, okay?"

"I surely will. Thank you."

"No, thank *you*, Uncle D. Happy hunting, now."

I could actually hear the big smile in his voice. I had an anxious moment wondering whether he could charge hookers to a hotel room in Denver. Guessed no. Didn't really matter anyway. Even if he ran the bill up to two thousand or so, it'd be worth it to have him out of sight and out of mind for the better part of a week. I was just about to hang up when he said, "One more thing."

Managed to keep my impatient sigh from going into the mouthpiece.

"What's that, Uncle D?"

"Just before you called I stumbled over something you might want to know. Can't tell you where I got it, 'cause it's not after midnight yet."

"Understood. I'm listening."

"The police have identified the burglar who broke into your office Saturday night as a Blackwater alumnus named Bart Reuter. Hell of a name for a burglar. Sounds more like a starting pitcher for a West Coast baseball team."

"I believe I read that this morning, Uncle D. Except for the Blackwater part, which is very interesting."

"He'll make his first court appearance sometime in the next hour or so. He is lawyered up. His lawyer's name is Sabrina Teitel."

"Well, as a matter of fact I did *not* know that." I scratched out a frantic note. "Thank you. That is most helpful."

"Well, it's going to get a lot more helpful. Two years ago Sanford Dierdorf had to appear before the general counsel of the Department of Energy and answer some sharp-edged questions. The lawyer who prepped him for that and sat beside him while he was doing it was Sabrina Teitel."

"Oh."

"You have a real good day now, Josephine."

Chapter Twenty-nine

Traipsed down to see Seamus. The carpet was no longer squishy-wet, but aside from that his office still qualified as your basic mess. Building Services and Seamus himself had done their best on Sunday to clean up the worst of the damage, but when you've had fire and rain inside the same office in five minutes, it's not going to look good as new overnight.

Didn't faze Seamus, though. I entered to see him sitting there at his desk, looking as pleased as an altar boy who got all the candles lit on the first try. And to see a gun right in front of him, dead center on his desk blotter.

Specifically, a handgun. Snub-nose revolver. Barrel maybe two inches long. Example of what liberals used to call "small, easily concealed handguns" in the days before the NRA got two-thirds of Congress in its hip pocket and the idea of someday regulating the things went to live with all the people speaking Esperanto.

"Have a seat."

Seamus gestured toward a guest chair whose cushion he'd covered with two file jackets, so that I could sit down without getting my Spanx damp. I perched gingerly on the blessedly thick paper. Seamus picked up the revolver. He did this rather delicately, holding the butt with his left thumb and index finger and bracing the muzzle against his right index finger.

"This is a Colt .32-caliber revolver. Do you know how to handle something like this?"

"It may be possible to earn a bachelor's degree in the State of Louisiana without acquiring a basic familiarity with firearms, but I don't know anyone who's ever done it."

"I'll take that as a yes." He put the gun down. "I've been thinking about that crack *Rotunda* made about us and the NRA."

"I believe that remark was a feeble attempt at satire rather than a serious suggestion."

"Even a blind squirrel occasionally finds a nut." Seamus beamed; not a good sign. "I want you to apply to the District of Columbia city government for a concealed-carry permit for this weapon."

"I see."

"We'll get a holster for you."

"Okay. That's very thoughtful."

"The store already has it on order. Picked it out myself from the catalogue. Nice little thing. Dark brown, supple leather. Goatskin, I think, instead of cowhide. You could clip it to your belt or, if you didn't want to actually have it on your body, it wouldn't take up much more room in your purse than a couple of packs of cigarettes. Since you don't smoke anymore, it's perfect."

"Seamus," I said, trying hard not to sound like I thought I was talking to a ten-year-old, "are you telling me that you've spent half the morning getting me set up to play Sam Spade's wife? I mean, for starters, what if they deny my permit application?"

"Oh, they'll deny the application, all right."

"I'm not sure I'm following this."

"Don't you see?" After favoring me with his pleading, frustrated artist look, he sort of gazed off into the middle distance with a dreamy expression on his face. "We make you the poster-girl victim of unreasonable gun regulation. A sixty-second TV ad with Josie front and center, brave and spunky. 'I was attacked by a vicious thug in my own office in the very heart of Washington, D.C. I was beaten and I could have been sexually assaulted or even killed. The next time it happens, I want the odds a little closer to even. And you know what they used to say in the old West: *God created man, and Colonel Colt made him equal.* But Washington, D.C. *will not let me protect myself.* When I applied for a concealed-carry permit, Washington, D.C., turned me down because they didn't think what happened to me was dangerous enough. The bureaucrats in Washington, D.C., are denying me my constitutional right to defend myself from murderous thugs.' Then the voice-over: 'Tell Congressman so-and-so to support legislation mandating accommodation of concealed carry for law-abiding citizens by every state and municipality in the country. If it happened to Josie Kendall, it could happen to your wife. Or your daughter. Or you.'"

The sheer genius of the idea left me almost breathless. You see, the way you pay the rent as an activist-fund-raising organization is to find folks with an agenda like yours, take money from them, give some of the money to people who can advance the agenda, and keep the rest. Mostly you give the money to techies and copywriters and actors and voice-over talent to make issue-advocacy commercials—you know, just like campaign commercials, except without the word "vote." Seamus was telling me he'd found a way for MVC to pay itself for copywriting and acting and maybe even voice-over. Throw a few bucks at camera guys and sound technicians working for scale *and pay ourselves everything else.* Gave me a glow just to think about it.

"Blows me away, Seamus. When it comes to creative, no one can top you."

"I know how you feel about the victim card." Seamus said this apologetically, almost sheepishly. "But Josie, this could get our foot in the door *with the NRA!* We could get a million-dollar buy-in for this in the next election cycle. Maybe two million—most of it straight to the bottom line."

Truth to tell, my not liking the victim card actually made Seamus' idea all the more appealing. I could negate the victim stuff by standing up there and doing a ball-buster Amazon number, Wonder Woman with a Colt .32 instead of a magic lasso. But Seamus apparently *thought* he needed to sell me on this, and in politics you never waste a misunderstanding. Shrapnel from Uncle D's last little bombshell was still rattling around in my head. I decided to see if I could do something about it.

"Seamus, you know that I'm a team player. But I'm also in a somewhat delicate situation. I will sign off on this with no problem at all—but there's just one thing I need to know."

"What's that?"

"Jerzy's pitch-file included a picture." I described the thing. "I'd like to know where your excellent nerds got it—because they sure didn't pick it up at last year's *Star Trek* convention."

He didn't blink. Didn't hesitate for a second. Didn't flinch.

"You will have that information by five o'clock tonight, even if I have to fire every goddamn one of them to get it."

At precisely three-thirty-seven p.m. I got the information.

"Not sure this was worth all the drama," Seamus said when he strode into my office. "I had to beg and threaten and swear and lie through my teeth. And you know how much I hate swearing. After all that, I was expecting to find out it came from the CIA or Mossad or something. Turns out we got it from an ex-fed supplementing his pension with a little private gumshoe stuff. His name is Theo McAbbott."

Chapter Thirty

"No kidding!" Rafe looked up from the round steak he was grilling on our patio and beamed at me with radiant delight. "Theo? Extreme telephoto lens, picture of an armed man taken from hiding? Seriously? That rascal! Didn't think he had it in him."

"Well, he did put in thirty years with the FBI."

"Solo covert visual surveillance is a step above standard field-agent gigs—especially with no back-up and no official cover."

I tasted my martini—*very* good—and considered Rafe's comment. An uncomfortable thought had been nagging at me, and I figured I might as well get it on the table.

"Are we sure he was off on his own? Any chance the Bureau might have brought him back in for one more case because he had special skills or something? 'Cause if he took that picture *for* the FBI, Tony won't have gotten many points for me this morning when he turned over the copy I made."

"Hollywood stuff," Rafe said dismissively. "When it comes to doing things by the book, the FBI makes the Marines look like Unitarians. No way they'd pull an alumnus off the scrap-heap to pitch in on a case."

"Makes sense, I guess. And I know a lot of retired agents sign on as security consultants with clients that have edgy business models. What with the three book contracts you got him, though, I wouldn't think Theo would have to beef up his pension with penny-ante stuff like that."

"I don't think he did it for money." Rafe flipped the mini-steaks and nimbly retreated from flames that flared off the siz-zling charcoal. "I suspect he did it to wake up his badge-and-gun memories, remind himself of what it's like to work on a real case."

"So that he could channel that into his writing?"

"Exactly, you Creole minx." Rafe saluted me with a long-handled spatula as I smiled at his little *nom d'amour*. "His hook is that he's writing from personal experience instead of just recycling *Law and Order SVU* scripts. When I looked at his first draft of the story we're working on now, I told him it had a by-the-numbers feel to it. Kind of generic. I suggested that he dig down for a little Theo-stuff. Maybe this was his way of putting some more stuff there to dig for."

"Did it work?"

"Whether it was this or something else, his prose got a lot more *real* after that. I think the one in the pipeline that we've been working on together might really ring the bell. Could be a break-out for him."

I stood up from the wooden deck chair where I'd parked myself. Took a little stroll around our patio, idly noting the red-pink-maroon variation of the flagstones. *It really is a Hell of a coincidence, isn't it? IF it's a coincidence.*

"You know what, honey?" I said. "It would be really inter-esting to know who Theo was working for when he took that picture. 'Scuse me. *Whom* he was working for."

"Just on a wild guess, I'd say he was probably working for Jerzy Schroeder, wouldn't you? I mean, a business rival and an ex-wife in the same picture? It's a small world, but not *that* small."

"So your loyal client and your adoring wife were working simultaneously but independently with a guy who got his brains blown out—and *you're* the one the police are investigating."

"Seems like there has to be a logical connection, doesn't it?" Rafe took a sip of his G&T. "If I were in a speculating mood, I'd speculate that Schroeder probably got your name from Theo. Schroeder approached you, not the other way around, right?"

"Right. That fits together. Be nice to pin it down, though."

Rafe scooped round steak onto buns on a platter that he'd set on a wooden platform attached to the grill. He put lettuce and tomato on mine and slathered his with steak sauce. I held out paper plates from a redwood table between the two deck chairs. He plunked one sandwich on each. As he completed that task he looked at me with gently raised eyebrows and spoke in a quiet, casual tone that triggers my *Listen up, girl!* reflex.

"Theo won't confirm that Schroeder was his client, but if he thinks we already know he might clear up the connection. Why don't we just call him and ask?"

Thought about it for a second, and damned if I didn't come up with the right answer.

"After we eat."

Don't know why but, looking back on it, that simple dinner seems like a little vacation from the whole mess. Just sitting there in the humid July night on those adjoining deck chairs on a patio that might as easily have been in Columbus, Ohio, or Madison, Wisconsin, or Atlanta, Georgia, as Washington. A happily married couple, comfortable with each other, Rafe maybe thinking about trying hard for YES on having a baby, me getting more and more comfortable with that answer. Or the other way around. Just *normal,* you know? No murder, no investigation, no damage-control strategy, no media hustlers to worry about.

I think Rafe had the same feeling. We kind of stretched the meal out, taking our time, as if we didn't want our little vacation to end.

It did end, of course. Took us over thirty minutes, but we'd finally eaten every crumb. While I policed things up, Rafe pulled out his phone and punched in Theo's number. Rafe's half of the opening banter ended with, "Let me put you on speaker as we're walking inside. Josie is here with me."

"Hey, Josephine Kendall! You keepin' it real, Empress?" 'Empress' because Napoleon's Josephine had Creole blood—a little tease that Theo started using with me after Rafe made him take it out of *Knuckle Rap.*

"Keepin' the balls in the air, Theo." I slid the patio door shut and locked it. "Listen, tiger, were your ears burning this afternoon?"

"They're *always* burning. Anything in particular?"

"Well, there's this picture." I described it. "My boss got it from a freelance opposition-researcher, and the oppo-research guy said he got it from you."

"Did he now?" Theo is a handsome son-of-a-gun, and from the way his tone changed I imagined him running his fingers through hair that he somehow manages to keep thick and inky-black even though he's in his late fifties. "Does this oppo-research guy have a name?"

"Probably, but I don't know it."

"Got it from me, huh? Well well well—what do you know about that?"

"Josie and I don't know a thing about it," Rafe said, jumping in. "But we were kind of wondering whether you might have some insights that you could share with us."

"I'll give that some thought. Say, you know, we haven't gotten together for awhile. I'm kind of pinned here in the house cranking out the latest masterpiece, but maybe you two could come down here Friday night for pizza and beer. We could talk about anything that comes up. How does that sound?"

Rafe arched eyebrows at me. I nodded.

"Sounds great, Theo," Rafe said. We'll try to make it by six-thirty or seven."

"It's a deal, then."

Rafe ended the call. We looked at each other. Didn't have to exchange a word. Theo had come through loud and clear: He wasn't sure how much he could tell us, but he for sure had something to tell.

Damage Control Strategy, Days 6 and 7

(the first Tuesday and Wednesday after the murder)

Chapter Thirty-one

Tuesday—boring. I spent most of it finding out what a pain in the butt applying for a D.C. concealed carry permit was going to be. A deal is a deal, though: Seamus had held up his end of the bargain, so I'd hold up mine. I told him I didn't see how we could get the application in until Friday, and he said that was just fine, feeding one of my own lines back to me: "It's more important to do it right than to do it fast."

Which brings us to Wednesday. Not boring. Wednesday was make or break for DeHoic and the Jerzy pitch-file deal.

Her geek-squad showed up first thing in the morning, Washington Standard Time, *i.e.*, nine-fifteen. Seamus told them to knock themselves out. One-hundred-sixty-three minutes later they called DeHoic with the news that we were cleaner than an IRS audit of a major campaign contributor: no file access after my chat with DeHoic (except mine, which I'd told her about), no file copying, no file forwarding, no file print-outs. In other words—Nice work, Josie.

DeHoic herself showed up twenty minutes later, lawyer in tow. DeHoic wore gray again, but this time a dress, and with a more age-appropriate hat. Same matching heels and gloves. The lawyer, thank Heaven, wore navy blue: pantsuit and pumps that kind of matched. Seamus led them to our conference room—also gray, but that was a coincidence—where I waited with my laptop open and my fingers itching to type.

Seamus and DeHoic went at it with each other for awhile in a mostly professional but occasionally badass kind of way. I took notes and the lawyer, as far as I could tell, provided decoration. The first time smoking came up Seamus explained how much he despised nanny-state nonsense like the D.C. Clean Indoor Air Ordinance but, shaking his head sadly, said that of course we had to respect its strictures. He figured that denying DeHoic nicotine would give him an edge in the negotiations, so the shameless scofflaw suddenly morphed into Mr. Civic Responsibility.

They started off miles apart on price, and it didn't look to me like they'd made much progress when DeHoic veered off into some of the non-price terms in the draft agreement Seamus had proposed. The first two or three went pretty fast, but then things hit a major snag.

"Why do I have to sign off on this blather about using the file to promote Jerzy's commitment to the environment?" DeHoic tossed her pen on the table in disgust. "No one is ever going to confuse me with Pope Francis."

"I agree. Not the slightest resemblance."

"I'm buying the file. Why is it anyone else's business what I do with it?"

"Because it might be evidence in a criminal case," Seamus said. "Therefore, I have to be able to show that we turned it over to you with the expectation that it would continue to be available, and that we would be surprised and disappointed if it turned out that the file was inexplicably lost or destroyed."

DeHoic pouted. Seamus waited. DeHoic spoke.

"You have a great deal of money riding on this."

"Not enough." Seamus shook his head. "Business is business, but prison is prison. You don't have enough money to get me to do a hundred hours of community service, much less go to the slammer."

"So you're saying this is a deal-breaker?"

"Yep."

I showed the room a poker face, straight out of the Rampart Street Casino in New Orleans. Inside my head, though, I was whistling in admiration of Seamus' bluff. *Pay attention, girl. You just might learn something.*

"Let's put this aside for now," DeHoic said. "If we can agree on a price, we'll circle back to it."

Sounded to me like a one-way ticket to nowhere. After all, they'd gone to the substantive stuff in the first place because they'd reached impasse on price. Seamus, though, smiled happily at her suggestion.

The second round of price negotiations was great, if you like that kind of thing. Real movement. DeHoic and Seamus had suddenly gotten serious. Had me on the edge of my seat. I probably could have sold tickets. Even so, it took Seamus a solid twenty minutes to get DeHoic within sniffing distance of half a million. I smelled climax when he went into his credibility riff.

"It's called 'credibility,' Ms. DeHoic." On the table in front of him, Seamus' thumbs and index fingers spun a shiny black oblong—the goods we were really peddling, in the guise of offering our creative issue-advocacy services. "End of the day, credibility and professionalism are all MVC has to sell. We can't slop out an issue-ad campaign with voice-overs that sound like they were done through tin cans connected with string. We need production values proportional to the importance of the issue."

"Yeah yeah yeah."

"By rights this should be a million-dollar campaign. Seven hundred thousand is really bargain basement."

"I'll throw you a fig-leaf. Five hundred ten thousand. Dollars, not euros." Seamus winced as if someone had gut-punched him, but DeHoic didn't seem impressed. "That's as high as I'll go."

Long silence. My mouth stayed firmly shut. Seamus' lips quivered. No way he'd walk away from the table with that kind of money sitting on it.

"All right," he said finally. "I'm not happy about it. We won't make a penny at that level after we've covered creative and production costs. But for Jerzy's sake I guess we can do business on that basis—*if* you accept the intended-use clause."

"Agreed in principle, but I need wiggle room." Abruptly standing up, DeHoic wig-wagged her right hand between her lawyer and Seamus. "You two work on it and get it done. I'm going out for some polluted air."

She turned her gaze to me. I got the message right away.

"Would you like some company?"

"I certainly would."

I figured the point of the break was for DeHoic to have a cigarette, but I only get partial credit for that one. We'd put a full block between us and MVC's building before she pulled her silver case out. She went through the motions of offering one to me, and she just shrugged when I murmured "No thanks." She took her time lighting up—not the way someone does it when they're desperate for a fix.

It was a beautiful day, for July in Washington. Temperature under ninety and humidity behaving itself. Puffy clouds in a blue sky. Walking felt great. When you peel away all the pretension and facades and self-importance, Washington really is basically a Southern city—maybe not as southern as Birmingham or Nashville, but every bit as Dixie as Richmond or Baton Rouge. Walking along like that reminded me of strolling down St. Phillip Street with Papa when I was eight or nine years old, before he got sick.

We stopped in the middle of the Arlington Memorial Bridge, leaned against the granite railing, and took in one of the views the tourists come for: Washington Monument, Jefferson Memorial, and the reflecting pool between the Lincoln and World War II memorials.

"I can't read you." DeHoic let smoke trail from her lips toward the Potomac. "I can't see the wheels turning in your head the way I can most people's."

"Thanks, I guess."

"Logically, I know you have to be thinking of some way to leverage this into a payday from Dierdorf. You're young and not as savvy as you think you are, so you just might be dumb enough to think you can pull it off. But I can't be sure."

"I have no idea of playing a double-game with you. As Louisiana's own Huey Long once said, an honest politician is someone who, once he's bought, stays bought. MVC is finished if word gets out that we betray paying clients."

"What would you have said if you *were* planning to fist-fuck me up the ass with Dierdorf before I was halfway back to New York?"

"Exactly what I just said, I guess." I turned an absolutely neutral expression on her. "But I would have said it with an earnest smile, and bobbed my head in a charmingly girlish way while I said it."

The smile she gave me for once seemed real. Had some warmth and depth to it. The barren womb apparently hadn't completely wiped out her capacity for genuine human connection. She reached in her purse, fished around like women often do, and finally came up with a much-folded piece of paper that looked pretty beaten up. She handed it to me. I unfolded the thing and studied it. Looked to me like a PDF printed off an e-mail.

"Flight plan for a Gulfstream two-eighty private jet," I said. "Hays, Kansas to Washington, D.C. Leaving at five o'clock in the morning on the day Jerzy was murdered." I memorized the aircraft identification number, just on the off-chance that it might match up with numbers in the improvised screenshot I'd taken.

"One of Dierdorf's main holding companies owns that plane. He's not on the passenger list, but he treats that plane like his own personal property. It doesn't fly anywhere without him."

"ETA D.C. area long enough before the murder to make setting up an ambush possible even after considering ground travel," I said after studying the flight plan some more. "Cutting it a little close, though."

"Oh, Dierdorf himself wouldn't have been the trigger-man. I've seen him hunt big game, or try to. It took him four shots to get one elk that just stood stock still, like the Helen Keller of quadrupeds."

"Then what's the connection? Why would he fly to D.C. that day?"

"Maybe he'd set up a meeting that Jerzy would leave his home to travel to, putting himself in a sniper's sights when he did. Where were you and Jerzy supposedly going when he stopped the bullet?"

"To see a key potential investor."

DeHoic looked at me for three long seconds, as if with a little silent encouragement I could connect the dots for myself. Then she apparently decided that another hint wouldn't do any harm.

"Which car were you going to take to the meeting?"

"My Ford Fusion."

"Instead of Jerzy's Infiniti or his Porsche."

"I buy American. MVC policy."

"It would make sense for Dierdorf to tell Jerzy to come to the meeting in a car that people wouldn't recognize as his. And I'm betting Jerzy told you to park on the east end of the house's long, curving driveway, where the hedge would screen your car from casual observers, instead of on the west end, near the garage."

I blinked. *How did she know THAT?* Then I nodded.

"That's why he took you out the back door and through the garden. That would be the quickest way to get to the east end of the driveway—*if* you started from the master bedroom on the second floor, and went down the back stairway to the kitchen."

I winced. Tried not to, but I couldn't help it. She looked back over the river, pretending that she hadn't noticed. A gull, almost pure white with a little blue-gray tinge on the underside of its feathers, seemed to hang in the air, wings spread but motionless, floating on the breeze with only the minimal, barely perceptible forward movement necessary to keep from falling.

"Beautiful, isn't it?" DeHoic asked.

"It truly is."

She took the flight plan back from me and refolded it.

"That isn't just a flight plan. It's an insurance policy in case things get too hot for your husband. 'Reasonable doubt' written all over it. So if I were you, I'd try real hard to keep me happy."

"I assure you I will bend every effort in that direction."

"Don't blow me off, honey. You're a decent girl, and you're not as dumb as you look. But you will be in way over your pretty little head if you start fucking around with Dierdorf. Plenty of taxpayer dollars could still stick to his fingers before that solar power boondoggle is played out."

"I hear you loud and clear."

She nodded at the gull, which seemed like it had hardly moved.

"That lovely bird floating elegantly on the air with such luminous grace while the sun glints evocatively from its wings—do you know what it's doing?" Without waiting for an answer, DeHoic turned to face me. "It's looking for something to kill."

Chapter Thirty-two

By the time we got back, Seamus and DeHoic's lawyer were finished and seemed happy with their work. DeHoic sat down next to her lawyer. Taking her time about it, she glared at the neat, Palmer Method handwriting squeezed into the margin of the draft agreement next to a printed paragraph that had been crossed out with a long, flat Z. She pored over it as if she were a rabbi parsing the Talmud.

"Why can't we say 'present intention'?" she demanded, looking up and locking eyes with Seamus. "What's wrong with that?"

"Because that would tell anyone who sees it that I knew you might have a different intention in twenty-four hours—which would defeat the purpose."

"I don't like it."

"Tell you what." Seamus smiled and spread his arms expansively. "I can have these changes incorporated into a clean draft in five minutes. I bet the words will look better to you in type."

"Skip it. No clean draft. We'll initial the changes and sign it as it is."

"That works too."

"But it's going to cost you. Since you're so scared of the cops, I get a bargaining-with-pussies discount. Four ninety-five. Say yes or I walk."

Seamus reached for the pen like it was the last cigarette on Earth.

Damage Control Strategy, Day 9

(the second Friday after the murder)

Chapter Thirty-three

"You know, miss, you can do this online."

"I do realize that, Ms. Robinson." I nodded earnestly at the gray-haired, African-American woman across the counter from me in a room sprawling over roughly a quarter of the John Wilson Municipal Administration Building's third floor. The white-on-beige nameplate in front of her read "Glencora Robinson." "But I thought I'd better come down in person because of the urgency of my situation, what with the break-in at my office last weekend and all. I really hope that you'll be able to expedite my application."

Pronounced skepticism colored the look she gave me. Outright hostility saturated the glare she gave Seamus. He had an inconspicuous digital camera trained on my encounter with this put-upon civil servant who just wanted to get to four-thirty p.m. so that she'd be one week closer to her full-pension vesting date. I was applying for a license permitting me to carry a firearm for personal protection and self-defense. Only my application or a bad case of constipation could have accounted for her painfully annoyed expression, and I'm betting on the application. If the Supreme Court hadn't dragged it kicking and screaming into a plain-meaning view of the Second Amendment, the District of Columbia wouldn't even let citizens possess guns in their own homes within city limits, much less walk around with the things.

Robinson clicked her eyes down to the application I'd filled out. She frowned at it, like an English teacher looking for sloppy diction. Mumbling to herself, she went through the copies of my birth certificate, driver's license, passport, and other attachments that were a big part of the reason it had taken me until Friday afternoon to get here. She looked back up at me.

"Did you report the break-in you talk about to the Metropolitan Police?"

"Yes, ma'am."

"Do you have a copy of the incident report prepared by the responding officer?"

"Yes, ma'am, right here." I produced it and pushed it across the counter through the opening at the bottom of the window.

"Hmm." Picking the single page up, she gave it critical scrutiny. "This says that the perpetrator was arrested."

"Yes, ma'am. My understanding is that he was released on bail earlier this week."

"Hmm." She paused. Then her face brightened. "We will need a certificate that you have completed a properly accredited firearms-training course."

"Yes, ma'am, I have that right here."

I slid that one through her window. Seamus and I had taken care of it the day before, at a place called Shooter's Paradise. Northern Virginia is lousy with accredited firearms-training courses, most of them sporting big NRA-Approved decals on their doors. I'd had to show that I could load the weapon safely, fire it properly, and clean it after firing it. Also that I was familiar with laws governing use of firearms, particularly about resorting to lethal force in self-defense. Ninety minutes flat. I'm a quick study, and the instructor had graded on a generous curve.

Robinson sighed. She assembled the collection of paper and tapped its bottom and sides on the counter to even them up. She busied herself for about seven seconds making a photocopy of the application's top page on a multi-use printer just behind her and to her right. She held the copy in a slot at the bottom of a large gray clock beside her. Something in the clock made a whirring-stamping sound. She passed the date-stamped copy back through the window to me.

"It appears that everything is in order." She didn't sound any too pleased about that. "That is your verification that your application is complete and has been accepted for filing and consideration this date. After appropriate review and verification, you will receive written notification of the disposition of the application."

"Thank you, ma'am. Do you know when I might expect to hear about being allowed to protect myself?"

"I will advise the appropriate offices of your wish for expedited treatment, but I cannot promise that you will hear by any particular date."

I gave her a pleading little pout that I'd worked on in front of a ladies' room mirror just before Seamus and I came over.

"It's just that, with the break-in and everything, I'm pretty concerned about my physical safety and I was hoping..."

That did it. Challenging her answer instead of just walking away after she'd dismissed me broke through the armor-plated bureaucratic caution she had built up over the years during her slow but steady rise from clerk-typist to her present position.

"I will advise reviewing officials of your request for special treatment," she said icily, saying 'special treatment' as if it were the kind of language that used to get kids' mouths washed out with soap. "But everyone who submits one of these things thinks they have to have a gun yesterday morning."

Seamus beamed. That sound-bite provided the icing on Friday's cake.

Chapter Thirty-four

Had a little bounce in my step as Seamus and I headed back to the office. Partly fantasies of *A Star is Born* with yours truly playing the lead, but mostly just TGIF. Main item on Friday night's agenda was pizza and beer with Rafe and Theo McAbbott, and I was flat looking forward to it.

Then just as I got to my office a call from Rafe snagged things up.

"You'll have to solo with McAbbott, babe."

"Why?"

"Matt Crisscuts is having a crisis of conscience."

"He has one of those about every six months, doesn't he?"

"Roughly. If he changes his position on abortion, his cable show will no longer be viable outside the womb. Or inside it, for that matter. So he's convinced himself that he can square the position with his religious faith. Then he sees a picture of himself as an altar boy or smells some incense or accidentally looks at a Planned Parenthood sting video, and he spirals downward. Bottom line, he needs an old buddy to listen to him while we drink all night."

Couldn't argue with any of that. As Papa used to say, pangs of conscience mean you still have a conscience, and that's good. Besides, when a friend needs you, that trumps everything else.

"Maybe we should just reschedule," I said.

"Can't see it. We need to feel out Theo about that picture before you debrief your Uncle Darius."

"True." Chewed on my lower lip for a second while I tried to figure out how to square the circle. Failed. "Okay, then. You and

Matt have yourselves a good night. I'll tackle Theo all by myself."

Wonder if he's gay. I know it makes me sound full of myself, but that thought actually crossed my mind near the end of my first half-hour on Theo's screened-in back porch Friday night. We'd eaten six slices of not-bad thin-crust cheese pizza between us. We'd had a Miller Lite each. And Theo McAbbott had not come on to me. Not even the first little off-color joke to get the ball rolling. Theo's only wife had divorced him more than ten years ago, and most of the time an unmarried straight male who isn't in holy orders will put some kind of a move on me if we're alone together for more than ten minutes.

Not Theo. So: *Wonder if he's gay?*

I had gone over the DeHoic/Dierdorf picture while we were noshing, getting non-committal nods and "uh-huhs" in response. With no intention of nibbling at either of the two remaining pizza slices, it seemed like as good a time as any to circle around to the excellent nerd's story about getting the picture from Theo. So I did. Theo took it totally in stride.

"That boy was telling the God's honest truth." Theo nodded emphatically. "I took the picture, and I'm the one gave it to him. And I'll tell you what: he made it worth my while."

"How in the world did he do that?"

"Oh, come on now." Theo's chuckle made the sides of his mouth and the outside corners of his eyes crinkle in a way that reminded me of Papa. "You're way too smart to think I can answer that question. Anything I'd tell you would have to be a flat-out lie. So why don't we just mark it as a no-comment and move on?"

"Fair enough. And you sure aren't going to tell me whom you were working for when you did the surveillance."

"Amen, sister!" Huge grin, punctuated by a hallelujah clap with his arms stretched way out, like you might see at a tent-revival.

"So, is there anything you can tell me?"

Theo did your basic U-turn and he did it in a big hurry. Face got serious, almost solemn. For two or three seconds I couldn't hear anything but the rotating fan behind me blowing evening air around, and frustrated flies bouncing off gray mesh screens. When Theo spoke he'd dropped the bantering salesman schtick and talked to me like I was just a buddy on the receiving end of an intervention.

"There is one thing I can tell you. One pretty important thing." He took a deep breath. "Sanford Dierdorf is your basic twenty-four-carat bastard. Bad guy. Any crime that pays well and doesn't require physical courage, he's game for it. He's fleeced taxpayers *and* investors fourteen ways from Sunday on at least three different projects. That solar power start-up that he's skimmed several million from is the least of his frauds—practically a sideshow."

"Sounds like someone your former colleagues at the Bureau might like to get their hands on."

"No inside information, you understand"—he winked—"but I will guarantee you that a task force of blue suits has had him on its to-do list for at least a year. Hasn't gotten any traction, though."

"Why not?"

"My guess is that he has friends with Schedule C appointments who see to it that requests for information about him from other federal agencies get slow-walked."

Whoa!

Schedule C appointments are senior positions in agencies made on political bases. Jerzy had wanted to get an investigation of Dierdorf's company going. But if the FBI couldn't get the responsible agency to take an investigation seriously, how could Jerzy have hoped to do it? So...what? So whoever hired Theo had leaked the picture to us through Theo, expecting us to get it to Jerzy without the fingerprints of Theo or his client on it. Why? So Jerzy could put it together with dope he already had—dope about Ann DeHoic, for example—and use it to motivate a GS 15 or two at Commerce or Energy or Interior or maybe even Homeland Security. That meant Jerzy hadn't hired Theo. So who had? And why was he—or she—so bashful?

"You look like you're getting a headache," Theo said as he stood and started picking up the pizza and paper plates.

Grabbing the beer bottles, I followed him through the back door into the kitchen. Typical bachelor kitchen: almost spotless, because it seldom gets used. Harvest gold. Really. There was something almost violent about the way Theo forced the pizza box's thick cardboard into folds and bent it over itself until it was compact enough to stuff in his recycling sack. Then he wrapped the two surviving pizza slices in aluminum foil—no Baggie; no wax paper; *guys!*—and tossed them in his refrigerator.

For the first time since he'd shown me in, I started getting an intriguing vibe from Theo, a little whiff of bad-boy/danger, sort of like the one I'd picked up from Jerzy, except dialed back about six clicks. Here was a guy who'd carried a gun on the job, put people in cuffs, maybe been shot at, probably roughed some folks up, or even shot someone himself. A little chill and a little thrill arm-wrestled to a draw in my belly.

"What I hear you saying," I told him as he rinsed out the beer bottles, "is that Dierdorf probably had Jerzy killed and wouldn't be shy about doing the same to me if I got in his way."

"Or if you started playing footsie with him."

Red flag. Chill just kicked thrill's butt. Theo was showing me a replay of DeHoic's warning/threat. If they were working together, this thing just got *way* more complicated. On the other hand, if they *weren't* working together and I'd been independently warned off by two pretty smart people, I'd better pay attention.

"Just out of curiosity," I asked, "where did 'playing footsie' come from? The only dog I have in this fight is my husband who has had cops crawling up his rectum since the day Jerzy went to Heaven."

"Or the other place." Theo did his aw-shucks grin one more time. "This might sound like a frat-boy line, but it's not. Would you mind coming down to my workshop in the basement? Something I'd like to show you."

Red flag *and* alarm bells. Looked in Theo's eyes. Question answered: *Not* gay. Tinge of lust in those shifty gray peepers for sure. Involuntary reflex; guys can't control it. Didn't mean he'd stop being a gentleman when we got downstairs, but…I took a breath.

"Sure, let's go."

Chapter Thirty-five

I expected to walk into a man cave with a wet bar and carefully positioned horizontal surfaces. Nope. Theo actually led me into an honest-to-Pete workshop. Dark gray concrete floor—clean, I noticed, which meant Theo thought this room was important. Weight bench and free weights against the far wall. A rig with a big round saw and other manly power tools that I didn't recognize dominated the room's center. And, over by the wall to my right, an oil-cloth-covered table with a rifle resting just above the table's surface on a couple of braces.

Near the rifle lay a scope, a set of mounting rings, and enough implements to fill up a standing tool box: a box of Q-Tips; what looked like a very long, very thin screwdriver; two silver-colored cylinders; a bottle of oil; a couple of miniature wrenches; one of those frames holding a transparent tube with liquid inside it that you use to see if something is level; a long, fist-sized pencil with an ultra-thin white lead point; and, just to top everything off, a small bathroom scale.

"Please tell me that rifle isn't a Winchester three-oh-eight," I said.

"It's not." Theo pulled a wooden, ladder-back chair up to the table and looked over his right shoulder to catch my eye. "Remington two twenty-four. Much higher muzzle velocity. Varmint gun. Prairie dogs, rabbits. Small things that are quick but don't need all that much killing."

"Okay." I parked my fanny on a red-lacquered stool against the near wall.

"What I want to show you is me mounting that scope there on this rifle."

"I'm watching."

"Get comfortable."

I am *not* going to lay out a blow-by-blow description of the mounting process, which went on for almost thirty solid minutes. Loosening and removing the eight screws in the mounting rings the first time he did it—three turns on one screw, then three on the one diagonally across from it, then three on the one directly across from that one, then three on the fourth screw, directly across from the first, then back to the first screw and so forth—took two minutes all by itself. And that was after putting his fingers on the scale to remind himself of what two pounds of pressure felt like, as he explained to me, so that he wouldn't over-tax the screws.

"These puppies are more delicate than a senator's ego," he muttered. "You can strip the threads on the suckers just by looking at them sideways."

He asked me to hand him a dowel, which I took to be the guy-term for what looked like one-third of a broom handle in the corner. I did. He fussed with that thing and the two rings a bit, then used the two metal cylinders to make sure he'd gotten the rings lined up right, and finally laid the scope gently in the cradles formed by the lower halves of the two rings.

But he wasn't anything like almost through. Used the Q-Tip to oil the screws before delicately screwing the top halves of the rings on over the scope, alternating among screws again, making the process look like open-heart surgery. When he finally set the screwdriver back down on the work bench, I exhaled.

"Done," I whispered, provoking a gently patronizing smile from him.

"Nowhere near done." He stepped back. "Come on over here and take a look through the sight."

I obeyed. Saw nothing but a blur at first. Then he turned a knob near the rear lens, and the paneled wall twenty-five feet away come into focus.

"You see that strip of Day-glo orange tape running down one of the grooves in that section of panel?"

"Yep," I said.

"Is the vertical bar on the cross-hairs lined up on it?"

"Pretty much."

"'Pretty much' won't cut it."

I got out of the way. He gazed through the scope. Grunted. Stood up straight. Drew diagonal lines across the mounting ring halves with the pencil, did some more open-heart surgery with the screwdriver, backed the scope up by imperceptible millimeters until the diagonal line on the top half matched perfectly with the diagonal line on the bottom half, then tightened the screws—again.

He looked through the scope again. He stood up and gestured toward the sight.

"Tell me what you see now."

I squinted through the coated glass.

"The vertical bar is lined up exactly on the tape, but they look like they're slanted just a little."

"It's your head that's slanted, not the bar. 'Canted,' the gravel guts call it. We know the tape isn't slanted, and therefore we know the bar isn't slanted. That's the important thing."

I stood up. He put the spirit-level—the frame with the tube of liquid in it—on top of the sight.

"Dead level," he said. "We won't need the wrenches. Thank God for that."

"That looked like a lot more trouble than I would have thought it was."

"Yep. Older weapons like Rafe's or this one, that's the way you have to do it. At least if you want it done right—and if it's not done right, what's the point?"

"Can't think of one, I guess."

He turned toward me. I could see sweat that had beaded across his forehead while he concentrated on mounting the scope.

"Someone who just wants to go out there on the first weekend of deer season and blow away Bambi's dad from a hundred yards, that's one thing. He can slop the thing together. Miss the first shot, he'll probably get at least two more."

"I'll have to take your word for that."

"But a single kill-shot for a human target at long range—different story, sister. That scope has to be in place *exactly*, without a speck of wobble to it. Has to be tighter than a...uh, well, tight as it can be. Say it like that."

I would have given anything to know what was supposed to come after 'tighter than a' before Theo remembered he was talking to a lady. At the moment, though, I had a more important question to ask.

"Point being—what?"

"Point being this: having a subscription to *Field & Stream* when you were a kid and going hunting with your drinking buddies once a year doesn't qualify someone for this gig. Mounting the scope right would be the easiest part of a professional hit, and *that* was plenty hard enough, as you just saw. Not the kind of thing someone takes care of during commercial breaks on *Meet the Press*."

Got it. No need to draw me a picture.

"In other words," I said, "Rafe didn't do it."

"Not without professional help, he didn't."

"Right." I managed a look of wide-eyed innocence straight from *The Sound of Music*. "Well that is a *big* relief. Because where in the *world* could Rafe have gotten professional help?"

Chapter Thirty-six

"...at a reception before the White House Correspondents' dinner. Big deal, right? Talking to Laraine Keesh, who I've known for, what, twenty years anyway. And we haven't been talking more than thirty seconds before I notice her looking over my left shoulder to see if she can spot someone more important than me to talk to. Twenty years! I mean, I don't know what it is. Like Washington has turned into some kind of giant frat party. What is it? Do you know what it is?"

Matt Crisscut's voice, coming from our living room. I heard it as I slipped, quietly as a water moccasin, into our kitchen through the back door after getting home from Theo's. Matt didn't sound slurred yet, but the bad grammar—"who" instead of "whom" and "me" instead of "I"—told me he wasn't completely sober, either. Glanced at my watch. Not even nine yet. Rafe had a long night ahead of him.

No sense trying for discreet, so I just made a grand entrance. Matt jumped up like I was his mom. Or long lost sister, anyway. Rafe rose a bit more sedately. Hugs, air kisses, squealed greetings, followed by the disclaimers I knew were expected of me.

"No, don't be silly, I don't need a drink. And 'adjourn to the basement'? Don't even think about it. You two stay right where you are. I have tons to do upstairs."

Exit Josie. Clean getaway. Up to our bedroom. Skirt, blouse, and pumps off; jeans, tee, and ballet slippers on. Fired up the iPad. Checked *Impolitic.* Nothing. *Daily Boot.* Nothing. *Inquisitor.* Nothing. *RealClearPolitics.* Nothing.

A snatch of Matt wafted upstairs as his voice got a little loud.

"...like one of those high schools in the movies where most of the kids are okay but there's this in-crowd of seven bitchy cheerleaders and a dozen inflated-ego jocks, and they poison the atmosphere for everyone. That's what Washington has become. That's what Washington is right now."

Okay. I guess. He was talking about me, of course. Not me personally, but all the twenty-somethings and thirty-somethings who'd come to Washington with calculation in our souls instead of stars in our eyes and let the serpent into paradise. Maybe he was onto something. Or not. Couldn't fuss with that now.

Checked *Rotunda.* Nothing. Checked my e-mails. Spam. Checked my phone. No messages, no texts. What next? Stream *House of Cards?* Or *Veep,* even?

I sighed. No. No way to put off thinking through the Theo-chat. Propped two pillows vertically against the headboard of our bed, leaned against them as I scooched onto the bed, and started parsing what I'd picked up.

Or would have started parsing it if a distracting question right out of left field hadn't popped into my head.

What would I have done if Theo had come on to me? Said no, that's what. *You sure about that, Josie?* Yes. Never gonna cheat on Rafe again. And I'm for sure never gonna get Rafe and myself mixed up in a big mess because I can't keep my Spanx on in mixed company.

Now, dammit, girl, *focus.*

Josie, you're a moral infant.

FOCUS!

I focused. Finally.

Theo had moved Heaven and Earth to convince me that Rafe just didn't have the skill set to have killed Jerzy. Really wanted to buy that, because I had a lot of trouble seeing Rafe as morally depraved enough to shoot a man from behind over adultery. Yeah, honor, unwritten law, man rules, I get all that. But what's honor got to do with bushwhacking a cad from almost a different zip code? Not exactly pistols at ten paces, is it? I didn't just love Rafe, I looked up to him, admired him. I wanted him to keep on being my hero.

The more I flipped the Theo coin, though, the plainer it was that it had two sides. What the alibi and Theo's gunsmithing demonstration and the other Theo stuff proved was that Rafe couldn't have killed Jerzy *without Theo*. So if the cops ever finished their eternal forensic audit of our accounts and failed to trace a huge chunk of our money into Theo's pockets, everything would be just peachy. But what if the audit showed Rafe *had* somehow paid Theo off? That would put my frivolous, thoughtless little fling in a whole different light, wouldn't it?

All of a sudden, I found myself in a Mirror Meeting. At Sigma Tau Delta, my sorority, a Mirror Meeting meant going into a quiet room with two or three sisters and taking a good, hard look at yourself; at where you were letting the sorority down and not pulling your weight and not living up to the ideals and all that stuff. With my head nestling back in the top pillow, trying to find a soft spot that was just right, I started that self-examination.

You messed up, girl. You flat messed up. True.

Right then I started missing Papa something fierce, like I hadn't in years. It had all happened so fast, that summer I turned twelve. Everything seemed fine, mostly, Papa just a little tired. Then he goes to the doctor and they run some tests. A week later he's in the hospital. Two months after that a priest is sprinkling holy water on his rosewood coffin. Pancreatic cancer. So fast. No time to get used to the idea.

All at once, right on the verge of my first period, the closest thing I have to an adult male in my life is Uncle D. A charming rogue, a brawler with blood on his bruised knuckles and the occasional broken nose, a hustler who'd show you a forty-five if fast talk and finesse didn't get the job done, a can-do Louisiana pol who viewed bribes as incidental sweeteners and payoffs as business as usual, an authentic scoundrel, true to himself, who'd smiled through the prison term when his chickens finally came home to roost.

A lovable rogue, but a bad dude all the same. A dangerous man, physically and morally. Can't you just imagine Freud getting his teeth into that one? "Father-substitute with no super-ego on the eve of pubescence? Nurse, hold my calls for the rest of the afternoon."

A little tear rolled down my right cheek, and I just let it go all the way to my jaw until it dropped off. I wanted Papa to show up magically and chew me out a little and then reassure me: *Josie, you're better than that. You're not a moral infant. You're a moral adolescent. You have a big heart and there's not a mean bone in your body. But you're impulsive and sensual. You go with what feels good right now and you don't think about the consequences. You messed up, for sure. You're better than that, though.*

I guess I could blame the bad-boy thing on Papa. Or on Sandy Jane or Nappy Lejeune or Charles Darwin or Sigmund Freud. But I think I'd better just blame it on Josie Kendall. Twenty-seven is about time to grow up.

Went ahead and had my cry. Nothing special. Just sort of wrung out the self-pity, kicked myself in the butt, and decided that I'd do whatever I had to in order to straighten things out.

And just like that, everything seemed real clear in my head. Real calm. Doubts all gone. Right then and there I knew that Rafe hadn't killed Jerzy over my affair. *Knew* it. No logic, no analysis, no assessment of probabilities, no mental spreadsheet, no decision-tree. I was just sure as I could be—"apo*dic*tically *certain*," as Uncle D might have put it if he were Dixie-pontificating in undiluted Henry Clay mode—that Rafe hadn't killed Jerzy for sleeping with me.

Okay. Felt a lot better. Still a big problem to deal with, but I was past the really hard part now. I'd call Uncle D tomorrow to debrief him, talk it over with Rafe, and go on from there. I was actually humming as I bounced out of bed.

The phone rang. Still humming, I answered it.

"Josie, this is your Mama. I'm here with Uncle Darius. We just got in from Denver."

We? WTF?

"Oh, Mama, hi. Listen, I was gonna call Uncle D tomorrow to see what he found out, and I was thinking we could talk then."

"We need to talk now."

"Well, okay, if you feel it's important." Chewed my lip, wondering how long I had before I'd have to drive Matt home—because neither he nor Rafe figured to be up to that chore. "How much time do you think we'll need on the phone?"

"Five more seconds. We're at Reagan National Airport. We need you to come get us. ASAP."

Chapter Thirty-seven

Dropping Matt at home sort of on the way complicated ASAP, but I got to Reagan National well before they had any right to expect me. All set to give the both of them a royal chewing out for just showing up out of the blue. But then, in my Fusion's bright dome light, I got a good view of Uncle D.

He looked like death warmed over. Mouse under his right eye. Stitches in his upper lip and the point of his chin. Big bandage on his forehead, right underneath where that scraggly hair that he wears over his neck starts. Overall skin tone kind of gray. He's a big guy—well over six feet and weighs close to two-fifty—and that made it seem worse. I noticed a featherweight cotton hospital pajama-top sort of peeking out from underneath the tie-less tan dress shirt he was wearing.

"Uncle D, what in the world—?"

"Later," Mama snapped. "We need you to get us to your place pronto. We'll talk there."

I managed that without too much trouble. Rafe, God bless him, doesn't get drunk often and when he does he's a neat and gentlemanly drunk—no getting sick on the kitchen floor or anything like that. He had gotten himself to bed by the time I got home with my unexpected company, so that took care of one complication. By around ten forty-five I had the four of us—me, Mama, Uncle D, and Jim Beam—installed around the glass-topped table on our deck.

"Denver Health Medical Center called me last night to tell me that Darius was in the emergency room." Mama had battleship-gray hair now, pulled back into a bun, and it bounced a little bit as she spoke. "I flew out there as fast as I could, praying just as hard as I know how all the way. Had to connect through Dallas, and that wasn't any picnic. Not something I would have done for anyone but kin. After Darius and I talked, I decided we'd better get face-to-face with you in a big hurry. So here we are."

"What in the world happened?" I asked.

"The chair recognizes Darius Zachary Taylor Barry," Mama said.

"Well, I did a little poking around, just like you asked me to. Turned up something interesting. It seems—"

"I meant the stitches and the bruises," I said.

"First things first," Uncle D said, sounding just a mite cross. "You see, that first part was easy. That conference was just crawling with folks who'll never send fan mail to Sanford Dierdorf. They say 'crony capitalist' a lot when they hear his name. They have lots of stories about him."

"Maybe you could tell us one." That would be Mama in no-nonsense mode.

"Well, it seems that the *po*-lice came to Mr. Dierdorf not too long ago because they'd found a firearm registered to him on the body of that fella got his brains blown out while he was strolling with you."

"You don't say."

"Dierdorf is just as breezy as you please about it. Says someone must be fiddling with serial numbers, because he carries his weapon whenever he legally can and he has it right now and here it is, take a look at it if you want. Well, turns out the weapon he showed those jack-booted fascists with badges had a different serial number than the weapon he'd been registered as buying and licensed to carry." Clearly enjoying himself despite the discomfort of his injuries and the numbing effect of whatever painkiller he was taking, Uncle D leaned back and sipped whiskey. "Even more curious, the weapon he produced was bought by someone else, many states east of Colorado."

"Holy sh—"

"You watch your mouth, young lady. Remember whom you're talking to."

"Sorry, Mama."

"So Dierdorf says the gun must have been switched somehow without his knowledge and he just hadn't noticed the trade. The jack-booted fascists are not overwhelmed by the plausibility of this speculation, but Dierdorf says that's my story and I'm sticking to it and you can talk to my lawyer if you don't like it. Or words to that effect."

I caught myself in time to say, "My word," instead of the first exclamation that came to mind.

"I heard this account, or something awful close to it, from three different gentlemen," Uncle D said. "And two of them weren't drunk."

"So looking at it from this Dierdorf cat's point of view," Mama said, "you can understand him wanting to get his hands on the file y'all had on what's-his-name, the decedent."

About now I expected Mama to pull out one of her mango-flavored Phillies Blunts and ask me to help her with it. They weren't exactly my cup of tea even before I quit smoking—nothing like as smooth as Rafe's Monte Cristos—but Mama doesn't smoke unless she's with other people who are also smoking. So, you know, filial duty, solidarity, all that stuff, I would share one with her, like Rafe had mentioned. When she didn't do it now, I figured Uncle D had been ordered off tobacco and Mama was abstaining so as not to rub his face in it. That's Mama.

"Okay, Uncle D," I said. "That dope about the handgun is serious stuff and I can't tell you how grateful I am that you dug it up for me. Now, tell me about how you got beaten up—and *don't* say you got up to relieve yourself in the middle of the night and walked into the bathroom door, 'cause I've heard that one before."

"Well, it was my own fault. In a way. You see, when I found it prudent to drop a name here and there while I was feeling these chatty gentlemen out, I would stick with one of my old favorites, Patti SuAn."

I groaned inside. 'Patti SuAn' is an anagram for 'Pantsuit.' Back before he went away, Uncle D actually managed to convince a reporter that it was the Secret Service codename for—well, you go ahead and figure it out. He ginned up a memo supposedly written by the President's chief of staff about something-or-other involving Patti SuAn, and then 'leaked' it to the reporter. By the grace of God it didn't go anywhere, but he's always been way too proud of it anyway.

"Uncle D, please tell me you didn't put out some cock-and-bull—"

"No, I didn't." His eyes twinkled for just a second. "That isn't my point."

"Get to what is your point," Mama said.

"I fouled up one time. Somehow let your actual name slip out. I'm awful sorry, honey. Can't think how I made a mistake like that. Guess I've lost a step."

"What happened?"

"Well, I let your name out around eleven o'clock Thursday morning. You know how conferences are. Word gets around real fast. By two o'clock Thursday afternoon I found myself in the company of a guy who wanted to chat with me about you. At length. A little rude about it, even for a Yankee. I realized what I'd done, so I begged off."

"And he insisted?"

"Not in the middle of the afternoon in the Denver Marriott City Center's bar, he didn't. But later that night, he or someone who smelled a lot like him, broke into my hotel room in a very insistent mood. Twenty-five years ago I could have mopped the floor up with him, but I'm afraid he got in more licks than I did."

I gulped. *Is this one on me too?*

"Uncle D, I don't want you to take this question the wrong way, because I realize the fix you were in—"

"Oh, you want to know how much I told him." Uncle Darius

chuckled. "Can't blame you for that. Fact is, though, I didn't tell him a blessed thing."

Didn't see how that could possibly be true, but I couldn't think of any decent way to say so. Lucky for me, Uncle D just kept on talking.

"You see, at the time this happened I was entertaining a young lady from Denver's adult entertainment sector. The guy who came after me made the mistake of breaking in before this sweetheart had been properly compensated. Real spitfire. Plus, she had a pig-sticker that Jim Bowie himself would have admired. She sprang into action in time to chase this gent off before he'd done any permanent damage."

"Well, thank the Lord for that."

"Amen," Mama said. Then she turned toward me. "I take it you understand now why we had to get to you right away about this—and why we didn't feel comfortable doing it on the phone."

"I do understand, Mama, and I am properly grateful."

"Now, seems to me we have to assume that this Dierdorf has a strong and unhealthy interest in you, just like Darius said. So we need to decide what we're going to do about that."

"Go to the authorities, for example," Uncle D said. "Or the jack-booted fascists, as I sometimes call them."

"I've already given the FBI a hint about him, but that was general. I don't feel right telling them that I'm a Dierdorf target until Rafe is cleared."

"I can see that," Mama said. "That Rafe of yours is a good man, and whether he did it or didn't do it, I don't want to see him fry for it."

"For sure." I thought that would be a more constructive response than telling Mama that her capital punishment metaphors are a bit out of date. "Unfortunately, I'm fresh out of ideas about anything else to do except keep my eyes open."

"I do have one idea," Uncle D said, after draining his glass.

Red flags. Alarm bells.

"What's that?"

"You make friends in prison, if you know how to do it. The friends you make have made friends in other places, and those friends have made friends. Know what I mean?"

"I'm afraid I do."

"Now, some of the friends I made have called me to see if I could help them out with this or that, and in several cases I have been able to do so. I'm betting that there's someone crooked who knows things about Dierdorf which no one at this table knows. I'm thinking you have a name or two in that category that you haven't shared with me yet."

"True."

I could feel myself blushing. Uncle Darius didn't have to spell it out for me. If I'd trust him with a name, he'd start going through his big-house alumni contact list and see if he could find someone who knew someone who knew someone who'd arrange an introduction. I looked Uncle D right in the eye.

"Danny Klimchock."

Damage Control Strategy
Days 10 through 16

*(the second Saturday through the
third Friday after the murder)*

Chapter Thirty-eight

I get a warm glow when I think back on the next week. Over the weekend Rafe and I did the hospitality thing for Mama and Uncle D while they rested up from their cross-country jaunt. That meant Josie going to Mass for the second week in a row, because the last thing I needed was some Mama drama. On Monday we got them on a plane headed back to Baton Rouge, so that Uncle D could start calling ex-cons from a phone that didn't belong to us.

Tuesday's highlight was Seamus taking me to a studio in Arlington, Virginia, to record our little skit on how Spunky-Josie needs to pack heat. Turned out to be a lot harder than I'd expected. I had the script cold, and the bit we were shooting wasn't supposed to run more than forty-five seconds, but we needed rehearsal and revisions and then take after take until Seamus and the digital video guy were happy at the same time. Finally got it done, though.

The idea was to post the thing on YouTube—not right away, but the next week if D.C. was still dragging its feet on my concealed-carry permit application. Get enough hits from gun lovers and Seamus could go to the NRA with his big pitch. Couldn't help feeling a little excited about it, even with all the drudgery. YouTube isn't exactly the big time—even if you go viral, you're doing the same thing dancing cats do every day—but humpty-thousand people were going to see my name and face and hear my voice so, hey, why not be happy?

Wednesday I started to get a little traction with the America-back-into-space thing. Got calls from the Congressman *and* the potential donor, both pretty upbeat. I started scratching out some ideas for a commercial that could be slapped together in time for the next primary season. I'd have to run the thing by Seamus, once I had something to run, but I already had visions of a modest six-figure score.

On Thursday came the call from Uncle D. He had good news.

"You should expect a contact from one Daniel Klimchock by early next week, sugar. Not sure what his angle is, but this is favors from, like, three guys. So if he's not what you were hoping for, let me down gently, okay?"

"Got it, Uncle D. Can't thank you enough."

"All right, sugar. Stay good, now."

Then came Friday. Epic day. Glorious day. A day to press in my memory book, or whatever the digital equivalent is.

First thing Friday afternoon I called Glencora Robinson, the hardworking D.C. civil servant who had reluctantly filed my application for a concealed carry permit, and asked for a status report. Made the call from Seamus' land-line, with him on an extension. He had a handkerchief over his mouthpiece, and worked so hard at keeping quiet that his face turned ripe tomato red.

"Your application is pending, Ms. Kendall."

"Well, it's been a week now and I've been coming to work blue-pencil scared every day, because of what happened and me being defenseless and everything. How much longer is it going to take?"

"I am very sorry about your fears, but I cannot give you an estimate for final action on your application."

Seamus broke into a gape-mouthed grin and pumped his fist in the air like the Redskins had just scored a touchdown to put them nine points ahead of the point-spread with two minutes left in the fourth quarter of the Super Bowl.

"Is there someone else I could talk to, then?" I asked. "You know, to try to explain why this is so important?"

"You're welcome to call anyone you wish to ask for an

appointment, but the civil service officers in this area are very busy with pressing affairs."

Seamus silently mouthed "*pressing affairs*" as his face lit up like a leprechaun's on St. Patrick's Day. He flashed an enthusiastic thumb's-up at me.

"Okay, I guess. Whom would I call, then?"

"I am not able to identify the particular civil service officer who has responsibility for your application at this point in time. That is a matter of internal deliberation and therefore is not subject to public disclosure."

I thought Seamus might wet his pants as he broke into his happy dance.

"Well, is there anything at all you can tell me, or am I supposed to just sit here and wait for this hoodlum to come back and take care of unfinished business?"

"I can only advise you to be patient as your application is considered in due course. You will be informed promptly upon final disposition. Please feel free to call at any time. We are here to serve the public."

She hung up. I hung up. Seamus let out a whoop they could have heard on Farragut Square.

"Did you get all that?" he asked, almost panting with eagerness.

"Every word." I gestured toward a computer screen with my telegraphic transcription of her answers underneath each of my scripted questions.

"'Pressing affairs.' 'Internal deliberation.' 'Here to serve the public.' That couldn't have gone any better if I'd written her lines as well as yours."

"Just out of curiosity, why didn't we record the whole call on tape? Then we could have laid an audio track on the clip with her actual voice."

"That might have been illegal. Taping a call without both parties' consent is a felony in Maryland, and who knows whether D.C. has a law like that as well?"

"Oh."

"Anyway, this will work just as well. Maybe even better." Seamus used both hands to frame an imaginary shot, and then put the first two fingers of his right hand on the thumb and ran it along the bottom of the make-believe frame. "We'll have a shot of you talking on the phone, with an audio track of you reading your lines and someone else reading this woman's. We'll make the audio track sound kind of wind-tunnelly, as if it really were a tape recording. We'll run a super along the bottom of the picture with a transcription of what's being said. In little tiny type we'll put, 'Actual conversation. Government employee's words read by paid performer from contemporaneous notes.' Have to take the time to do it right, so we'll spend Monday on the recordings and go live first thing Tuesday morning. Bet we get ten-thousand hits in the first eight hours."

And that was just Friday's opening act. The feature attraction came that evening, a little after six, as Rafe and I were just getting into our cocktails. Rafe's lawyer called. Rafe put him on speaker.

"The forensic audit of your accounts is complete," he said. "Bottom line: nada. Dry hole. Unless you spent the last twenty years accumulating ten gold bars that you've had stashed in a safe and you somehow got those to McAbbott, there is simply no way you could have paid him off."

"So I'm no longer a target of the investigation?" Rafe asked.

"Not a target. You'll be a possible suspect until the cops actually convince themselves that someone else did it, but every lead they had on you has brought them to a dead end. They're not going to spend any more taxpayer dollars going after you unless they just stumble over something new on their way to lunch."

"That's great news, Mike. Thanks for calling with it. Nice work."

In an instant, Rafe looked happier than I'd seen him in weeks: unforced smile and a relaxation of his upper body, as if he'd just unbuttoned a vest that was two sizes too small. Gave me a thrill just to look at him. Not sexual. I was just so happy for *him*.

As Rafe punched the OFF button on our phone console, I noticed a red light blinking. We had apparently gotten a call while Rafe and his lawyer were talking. Lightheartedly, with some happy-go-lucky, what-the-Hell body language, Rafe pressed the button to play back the recorded message.

"My name is Danny Klimchock. Someone asked me to get in touch with Josephine Robideaux Kendall at this number." He said my name haltingly, as if he were reading unfamiliar words from a scrap of paper or a PDA screen. "Bit of a problem. I'm heading overseas on Tuesday, connecting through Dulles with a seventy-five-minute layover. I'm supposed to land at Dulles at ten-twenty-five in the morning. If you can figure out a way to get through security, we can hook up then. Otherwise I'm out of pocket for a week. So, one way or the other give me a call at the number on your caller ID screen."

The voice sounded dead ordinary. No particular regional accent, no rasp, no growl, no unusual cadence, no hint of threat or toughness—or cordiality, for that matter. Smooth enough, but without the upbeat, forced charm of a telemarketer. A CPA's voice, or a Department of Transportation careerist's. I wrote down the number he'd called from, including the area code: three-one-two—L.A.

Rafe raised his eyebrows at me.

"One of Uncle Darius' friends came up with a Klimchock contact?"

"Sort of. Friend three or four times removed."

"Not exactly making it easy for you, is he?"

"Nope. But, as Uncle D sometimes says, food tastes better when you're hungry."

Damage Control Strategy, Day 20

(the third Tuesday after the murder)

Damage Control Strategy

Day 20

(the third Tuesday after the blunder)

Chapter Thirty-nine

The first 'Like' for our video came thirty-seven seconds after go-live at nine a.m., Eastern. The first 'Share' came six seconds later. You can't type as fast as you can point and click, so the comments didn't begin until 9:02. The first five pretty much captured the general tenor:

> "You go, girl! Shoot first and never mind the questions!"

> "Good luck, little lady!"

> "America needs rational gun control! The blood of innocents is on your hands, you trigger-happy bitch!"

> "Come to Texas! Y'all will have your permit before you're all the way off the plane!"

> ".32? .32????? Shoot someone with a .32 and all you do is make him mad! Get yourself a .40 caliber S&W semi-auto, and use 165-grain ammo. NOT 180 GRAIN! And shoot for the guts!"

That last one brought me up a bit short. This troll knew I'd applied for a permit for a .32-caliber weapon. Not exactly a state secret, of course: my application was a public record, accessible online. But apparently one look at my spunky face on a computer screen had stimulated this guy in Whoknowswhere to Google his way into the database and get detailed information from that application. A little creepy, for my taste. A girl likes attention, sure, but there's attention and then there's stalker-level obsession. A cold chill ran up my spine—and not in a good way. *Seamus, what did you charm me into signing on to?*

I picked all this stuff up on my way to Dulles, where I planned to meet Klimchock. Getting myself on the gate side of security? No problem. I'd be flying to Phoenix in September for the annual CCC Conference: CCC standing for "Calcatraveamus Cunes Caerulius," which is pidgin Latin for "Let's Kick Blue Butt." Bought a refundable ticket on a Delta flight leaving Dulles for Phoenix today. Printed out the boarding pass, sailed through security with nothing but a computer case for luggage, and here I was. After meeting with Klimchock I'd reverse course, trade in the unused ticket for one that would work in September, and not even have to pay a change fee.

By that time I had less than half an hour before Klimchock's ETA. A Starbucks cart at the west end of the gate area had me salivating. Unfortunately, Starbucks is on MVC's naughty list because it donates to Planned Parenthood, which is radioactive for a lot of our clients. Don't necessarily drink that particular Kool Aid myself, but the customer is always right—at least until I have that West Wing office. I figured that as sure as I decided to sneak a vente mocha, thinking no one would ever know, the CEO of one of our biggest donors would stroll off a jetway and catch me red-handed. So I trekked to the other end of the terminal where I found a pastry cart selling just regular, you know, *coffee*. Didn't taste all that bad, didn't cost four-seventy-five, and it got the job done. *Hmm.*

I'd just about finished it when Klimchock's plane pulled up to the gate. A little web research had told me roughly what he looked like but I came *this* close to missing him; turned out that web photo was a mite flattering. Not homely or anything, but most of his buzz-cut hair was gone, with just little gray tufts sprinkled here and there on his scalp. Bit of a stoop that you wouldn't expect in a guy in his late thirties; maybe several months in a Russian prison does that to you. Nondescript blue sport coat and khaki slacks with a dress shirt. No necktie. Smiling, but kind of a cockeyed smile that had a wariness behind it: *whatever you're about to say, I've heard it before.* He carried the kind of black attaché case that an employer might give you but that almost no one would buy for himself.

He spotted me about the same time I did him, but he pretended he hadn't. Flicked his eyes away real fast, the way men to do when a woman catches them staring at her cleavage. Probably didn't want to tip me that he'd looked me up. I acted like I hadn't noticed and approached him from his left with a peppy, "Mr. Klimchock?"

"You have to be Josie Kendall." Shifting his attaché case to his left hand as he pivoted toward me, he extended his right hand. I guess widening his eyes was his idea of faking surprise.

"Sure am!" We shook. "Thank you *so* much for taking the time to meet with me."

"Any friend of Jerzy's." He *almost* winked, but not quite. "Where did you get that coffee?"

"Far end," I said, gesturing east with my cup hand. "But there's a Starbucks cart on the other side, if you'd prefer that."

"No thanks." He shook his head firmly. "Joseph Stalin will get out of Hell before I pay five bucks for coffee. Besides, Starbucks donates to Planned Parenthood."

HELL-o. Seriously?

I know plenty of wealthy conservative fundamentalists. Deeply religious and just as sincere as a little girl with her first kitten. They're already saved, the way they see it, and they can't be unsaved no matter what, but they'll put in Saturdays on Habitat for Humanity projects anyway because Jesus loves them and when they do that it makes Him happy. If it weren't for people like that, I might have to get an honest job. But I didn't know any who'd *made* their money quite the way I figured Klimchock had made his.

Hmmm.

Before long we had our legs under a mini-table, with a cup of coffee and a croissant in front of Klimchock. About then— *boing!* My feminine sonar pinged to confirm that I'd excited male desire. Klimchock closed his eyes before biting into the croissant. Not sure whether he was saying grace or asking for help to keep from lusting after me in his heart. Whatever, when he spoke he was all business.

"First I thought Jerzy had cheated me. Then I thought he'd conned me. I finally realized that he'd just conned himself. A million bucks actually did end up being half of all that was left out of one-point-two billion in cash flow that our venture had generated over not quite two years. Putin made money, the KGB made money, a boatload of Russian bureaucrats got rich—and Jerzy and I barely covered our costs, with a couple of nickels left over to help us remember the ride."

"How do you mean 'conned himself'?"

"It's Russia." Eyes shining, Klimchock looked the way I suppose conquistadors did when they glimpsed El Dorado over the horizon. "There's just *so much* of *so many* things there: oil, natural gas, sturgeon eggs, small arms, big arms, really big arms, priceless art, diamonds from countries that aren't allowed to sell diamonds, opium from Afghanistan, tin and manganese and bauxite and uranium and metals you've never even heard of from countries under forty-seven different kinds of trade sanctions. And it's the Wild West! Wide open! Permanent boomtown! It seemed so easy at first. We figured that by my second quarter in-country we'd be clearing a million a month. *A month! Clearing!*"

"And you're saying he didn't just sell you that story, he bought into it himself."

"Totally. He and I joined a very big club. Germans, Eastern Europeans, Frenchmen, Armenians, Greeks, Turks, Americans— and plenty of Russians. You just *look* at the stuff and your eyes light up. You know the risks, you know the government is basically a gang of thieves, you know how other guys have gotten taken. But you think, 'I'm special. I'm smart. I'm savvy. I'll be careful.' You try to hustle Russia—and you end up like most of the others. Better than a lot of the others in our case. I got out with a whole skin, and Jerzy didn't hurt anything except his feelings."

"Jerzy had mentioned…higher numbers to me."

"Yeah, that's Jerzy." Big grin. "*Was* Jerzy. His memory came equipped with a telescope that enlarged everything he looked back on."

"So him trying to shift federal solar-power grant money away from Sanford Dierdorf to a wind-power deal he had arranged— was that just Jerzy fantasizing?"

"Not necessarily. That sounds real enough. No federal agency is going to leave one penny in appropriated funds unspent. If Jerzy had forced them to take the money away from Dierdorf, they would have looked for another place to spend it fast, and if Jerzy was sitting right there he'd be a prime candidate for it. But if that's what he had in mind, he couldn't let any grass grow under his feet."

"Why do you say that?"

"Because Dierdorf's scam was approaching its sell-by date. As soon as a new administration comes in and gets its act together, the hustle is all over. Whoever Dierdorf's rabbi is at the federal agency goes over to K Street to be a lobbyist, a new group of senior political appointees takes over, the GS-12's who've been biting their tongues come out of hiding—and when that happens, stick a fork in Mr. Dierdorf 'cause he's done."

"So even if Jerzy had gotten an audit started, the whole Dierdorf thing might have been history, even before the audit was finished?"

Klimchock thought about that, chewing meditatively on flaky bread as tiny crumbs drifted from his mouth to sprinkle his shirt.

"Have to go with yes on that one. Maybe Jerzy figured he could scare Dierdorf off just by getting something started; pull the cash switch before administrations changed; then make a quick buck for a year or so as the new kid on the block. Say two or three million. Nothing to sneeze at. Sounds like a long shot to me—but Jerzy was always an optimist."

"Do you think Dierdorf would have killed Jerzy to keep that from happening?"

"Sure, in concept. Hard to make the cost-benefit work, though. A contract-kill is a big risk and a big expense, and Dierdorf would only be protecting another twelve, fifteen months' worth of grant money. Dierdorf can be dumber than a box of rocks, though, and I suppose he might have talked himself into it."

"And then talked himself into having someone burglarize MVC's office?"

"I read about that." Brushed crumbs from his shirt and gulped coffee. "Someone named, what, Reuter?"

"Bart Reuter, yeah. Who lawyered up right away with a D.C. attorney Dierdorf had used before."

"Repeat business is the key to success." Klimchock shook his head slightly and grinned. "My take on that one is, you might pin the hit or the heist on Mr. D, but you can't make him take the rap for both."

"Not sure I follow."

"*If* Dierdorf killed Jerzy, then there's no way he sends a mouth-breather to town for anything remotely connected to that murder. He may be dumb, but he ain't crazy. No-necks have a habit of getting caught, and when they get caught they have a habit of talking."

"Well," I muttered, "Reuter is one for two."

"You sound a little frustrated."

"I am." I nodded. "Smart people tell me Jerzy was using me in some kind of bigger scheme, somehow, and maybe the using part hasn't stopped even though Jerzy is dead. No one can come up with a theory for Dierdorf that makes sense, though—and who else is there?"

"Well, there's me—but that kinda thing isn't my gig anymore. I had some time to think while I was behind bars in Russia. The main thing I thought was, 'If I get out of this alive, I'm finding something steady with a 401k plan and no chance of ever eating black bread and borscht again.'"

He fished a business card out of his shirt pocket. Orange on white:

KLIMCHOCK HYDRAULICS AND THERMODYNAMICS
Applied Engineering and Product Applications
"We're in the Solutions Business"

"This is my latest line. Should have the website up by the end of the week. I'm an engineer. Engineers are boring, but they mostly die in bed."

I took the card, thumbed it, briefly noted that the addresses and phone numbers below the headline stuff were Idaho, not L.A. An italic line across the bottom jumped out at me: *A Christian Based Company.*

"I hope this was helpful." Klimchock said this with an air of finality as he glanced at his watch.

"It was. Real helpful. Thanks again."

"Like I said, any friend of Jerzy's…"

This time he actually did wink. He gathered his things, sharing a friendly but superficial salesman's smile as he did. Right on the verge of sauntering away, he paused, hesitated, then offered a final comment.

"I just remembered something about a rent-a-thug named Bart Reuter. I heard he'd done some work for Dierdorf but hasn't had a Dierdorf gig since he blew a handoff from a bag-man in South Dakota over a year ago. Fracked it up, you might say. I'm having trouble seeing Dierdorf behind Reuter's escapade here."

Well, Josie, this just isn't getting any clearer, is it?

I called Uncle Darius on my way back to my car, because I just *had* to talk to someone about Klimchock. Darius came across as skeptical.

"So a guy who thought a million-dollar payoff for two years' work was chump-change found Jesus in the gulag?"

"That's what he says. I mean, it's possible. Maybe he really did just add things up and decide to make a quiet, decent but modest living as an applications engineer working out of a small office in Idaho."

"Right," Uncle D said. "And maybe you could be sincerely born again and still talk about murdering someone in cost-benefit terms, as if you were deciding whether to buy a software upgrade."

"Yeah," I admitted, "that bothered me a bit. I could see using an applications engineering business as a front—but why fake the born-again stuff?"

"Well, darlin', all I can do is speculate. If you wanted me to speculate, I would say that 'hydraulics' and 'thermodynamics' covers a broad field with a large number of specific applications that involve United States Air Force procurement officers. And if you wanted instant entrée with a fair number of Air Force officers, especially out west, faking a born-again schtick wouldn't be a bad place to start."

"Yeah, I can see that."

"Which doesn't necessarily mean Klimchock was into anything shady," Uncle Darius said. "You get the right buddies in procurement, you can make plenty of money without breaking law-one. Maybe noodge past a regulation here and there without exactly turning a square corner—but everyone does that, right? But you can also go for a lot more if you're willing to take the risk. At any given moment you'll find two or three gents in Leavenworth who can tell you all about it."

I probably sounded a little distracted as I thanked Uncle D and signed off the call. I couldn't help thinking that if Klimchock *was* faking the Righteous Christian stuff, that would put him in a place a lot like one I've been in from time to time.

My phone buzzed. Text from Seamus:

> NRA coming in pants over tease! Nd 2 follow ↑ ASAP!

Right now, for example.

Chapter Forty

Standard Beltway back-up for a weekday, with lots of people getting a head start on National Drive Like a Moron Week, so I found
myself looking at a solid forty minutes for the modest hop from
Dulles to MVC's office in northwest D.C. Had to call Seamus
back, of course. Happier than a Kardashian at a trunk sale, that
was Seamus. Up to his ears in plans for the biggest campaign of
his life, the campaign that wouldn't just take him to the next level
but to three levels beyond that; the equivalent of going from one
more competent college basketball coach to a coach suddenly one
win away from the NCAA title and a chance to play at the big
table for the rest of his career; a shot at changing his life forever.
He told me that as soon as I made it in, he and I would go balls to
the wall on Message Management, Measured Ramp Up, Rhythm
Discipline, Take Off Stage, Momentum Maintenance, and a
couple of other things. Seamus saying them all together suggested
a virgin with OCD seducing a nymphomaniac.

Following the Seamus call came three minutes of blessed
silence, broken only by a couple of naughty expletives provoked
by clueless Beltway driving. Gave me space to think. I wasn't
any too comfortable with thinking right now, so I called Terry
Fielding. Time to throw another bone to our designated media
whore. Got voicemail.

"Terry, Josie. Got something that I think would have to be off
the record but it might be helpful anyway. You have the number."

Two more minutes. Thought about turning on the news but didn't, because I figured it would be mostly about e-mails and I'd gotten to the point where hearing about e-mails made me sick to my stomach.

Four chimes: incoming call. Quick, technically illegal glance at the screen: Tony, my lawyer. Put him on hands-free.

"Is this a good time to talk?"

"Sure. What's up?"

"Two things. Related to each other. First, committee counsel has finally made a first, tentative overture about whether there's some way to tie that break-in to the Democrats."

"Sure. All we'd have to do is lie."

"Yeah." Tony's voice sounded languid, and I imagined him crossing his legs at the ankles and putting his feet up on the corner of his desk as he leaned back in his old-fashioned, tufted leather, swivel chair. "I explained that, and I was the second lawyer staff counsel had heard it from, so apparently MVC's counsel has explained it as well. But they'd still like an in-depth look into what the whole thing was about so they can make their own judgment."

"I assume we're going to slow-walk that," I said. "Start with a backgrounder at maybe the fifty-thousand-foot level."

"Right. MVC's counsel is drafting that."

"Good. 'Cause I'm sure not interested in paying you to do it."

"But you can only slow-walk something for so long."

"Okay. Then we start making noises about pending criminal investigations."

"Uh, yeah." Tony's voice no longer languid. "That's the second thing."

"Less tease, more—uh, 'more matter, less art.'" Caught myself just in time on that one. Channeling Uncle Darius all of a sudden.

"The prosecutor in the burglary case called. He wants victim input on a possible plea bargain."

"Well I'm a reasonable person. As long as they cut off one his hands, I'll go along with it. Even if it's just his left hand."

"Uh, yeah." Tony chuckled to show that he knew I wasn't serious. "Technically, we can't do that in this country."

"Since when? I thought President Obama had adopted Shariah law for D.C."

"That was just a rumor started by your friends at CCC." Chuckle. "The terms they actually have in mind are ninety days on work release and two years probation. For first offense non-violent attempted burglary, that's actually pretty steep by D.C. standards."

"Work release for a *burglar?* I mean, his *work* is stealing things."

"Focus, Josie. You're paying me a lot of money to appreciate your dark sense of humor."

I focused, all right. *Blinding* insight. Came in a flash, all at once, the whole package, no doubt about it. The NRA pitch, the proposed plea bargain, and the request from the committee all became well-machined components that I fit together effortlessly in my head into a humming, perfectly functioning spin machine. I swear, at times like this it is so *wonderful* being me.

"Tony, here's where we want to end up. We want them to offer that plea bargain, or something like it, but *over* my objection. We don't want the case to go nowhere for X months until Reuter jumps bail. We want it resolved, sooner the better, but with me on the record against the resolution *even though* it's the resolution we want. How do we get there?"

"Take an extreme position. Say we won't be happy with any sentence short of eight months net hard time, all on the inside. No work release, no good time, no weekend privileges. No way that will ever happen, so they'll cut us out of the negotiations."

"And what if we hint that a Congressional committee has a potential interest in this guy?"

"In that very unfortunate case," Tony said soberly, "the District of Columbia authorities will do everything in their power to wash their hands of Mr. Reuter as fast as they possibly can."

"So we get what we want, the committee gets blamed for mixing politics with justice, and the committee blames the prosecutor for gumming up its investigation. Perfect. We have a plan. And I expect a discount on this one, because I did most of the heavy lifting."

Tony seemed a little dazed when he signed off. Maybe *dazzled* would be a better word for it. Didn't have time to revel in my brilliance because my phone immediately rang again. Terry Fielding. Kept it on hands-free.

"Why would it have to be off the record, whatever it is?"

"Because there's only one possible source for this particular 'it,' so 'deep background' wouldn't really fool anyone," I said.

"Well, if 'it' is that the cops have finally finished tracking their flat feet through your money and accounts, there might well be another source for it. One but not two. Yet."

Political reporters' basic rule: If your source has a name you can print, then one is enough. If you're using anonymous sources, though—'a person close to the investigation', 'someone familiar with the facts but not authorized to speak publicly'—you need two. At least. And they have to be independent. So Terry was coming through to me loud and clear.

"So, if I were to tell you that we understand they've wrapped up the accounting stuff, I'd just be corroborating something you know independently."

"I'll take that as corroboration. How about corroborating that they didn't find anything?"

"All I know is that there was never anything to find, so what you say comes as no surprise."

"Ooh, nice one. You might have a future in this business, Josie."

I spent the rest of the day taking notes—*lots* of notes—while Seamus went over his grand strategic plan: Multi-million-dollar NRA campaign for uniform federal concealed-carry standards and licensing in any jurisdiction that failed to act on license applications within 10 days.

"Do you think Fox News will call it 'Josie's Law'?" I asked.

"Only if you get killed. And that's something I wouldn't ask of you." Big smile. "Which reminds me. You and I need to sign up online for NRA memberships before lunch."

Damage Control Strategy, Days 21 and 22

*(the third Wednesday and the fourth
Thursday after the murder)*

Chapter Forty-one

Seamus and I spent a lot of Wednesday on conference calls with NRA guys—and maybe one gal. They were all really happy, and the dimmer ones were pleasantly surprised, to learn that Seamus and I were both NRA members. I imagined these folks carrying big pistols in shoulder holsters under their three-piece suits or strapped to their waists over cashmere slacks as they sat around mahogany conference tables in wainscoted meeting rooms with assault rifles in gun racks mounted on the walls.

"Not 'concealed carry,'" one of them interjected early on. "'*Constitutional* carry.'"

Right.

The discussions seemed tentative and exploratory at first, with hints of skepticism about whether Seamus' idea really warranted "a big spend," as one of them put it. By the third conference call of the day, though, the NRA folks were doing a great job of selling themselves on the idea. They kept launching into rapid-fire chats with each other that seemed to treat Seamus' proposal as almost a done deal.

"We have a draft bill yet?"

"Guy from one of the Dakotas—what's his name, Wilcox or something?—sent one over yesterday. Piece of shit. Got the lawyers working on it now."

"Sponsors?"

"We could have sixty co-sponsors in the House and eight in the Senate within twenty-four hours."

Don't think I've ever seen a facial expression combine serenity and contentment so perfectly as the one on Seamus' puss while this back-and-forth went on. Finally a question came through for him.

"What's the timing on your next impulse?" He meant when would we post the next video.

"Monday." I could tell Seamus had pulled that one right out of his posterior.

"Can you get us a preview by first thing Friday morning?"

"Can do." The absolute confidence in Seamus' voice contrasted a bit jarringly with the panic written all over his face—but our potential client couldn't see the panic.

So we killed a lot of Thursday at Shooter's Paradise in northern Virginia. Our next post would have to punch up the visual ante from the first one. Josie having an exasperated phone conversation with a civil servant wouldn't exactly fill that bill. That meant a trek to the indoor shooting range in the back of the store. Opening shot of the .32 in its brown leather holster and, next to it, a yellow box of Winchester .32 caliber ammunition. The props sat on a rough-hewn wooden shelf a little over waist high. I started speaking from off-camera.

"My name is Josie Kendall. This is my weapon." My hands drew the revolver. "I bought it for my own protection after I came face to face with a thug who'd broken into my office in downtown Washington, D.C. He was arrested, but he's already back out on the streets."

Now all of me—not just my hands—turned to face the camera, holding the gun between my breasts, in both hands, with the muzzle angled toward the ceiling.

"If there's a next time, I want to be ready. I need to be ready." I deliberately but efficiently loaded cartridges into the cylinder. "I know how to load this weapon. I know how to clean this weapon. I know how to aim this weapon. And I know how to fire this weapon."

Snapped the loaded cylinder into the frame. Turned away from the camera and focused on an outline of a life-sized human figure, black lines defining arms, legs, torso, and head on slick white paper, with a bull's-eye target where the heart would be. Squeezed off six shots at one-second intervals. Got the torso with every shot. Not what you'd call a tight group, but an assailant with that much lead in him would be all through assailing for awhile.

Camera pulled back to focus on me. Turning to face it, I spoke as I snapped the cylinder out and used the spring-rod at its center to push the empty shells out. They made a nice, serial clatter as they bounced off the concrete floor.

"But the District of Columbia won't let me protect myself. My permit application is still pending after two weeks. The thug who attacked me got out of jail a lot faster than I can get someone to act on my permit application. I just hope they issue the permit before it's too late."

There. Done. Forty-five seconds of screen time. Between rehearsal, set up, flubbed lines, and multiple, from-the-top do-overs, we needed almost five hours to get it recorded. I swear that Seamus loved every blessed minute of it.

Chapter Forty-two

I read Terry Fielding's article online when I got back to the office. Didn't seem like all that much at first:

SCHROEDER MURDER INVESTIGATION GOING NOWHERE — OR SOMEWHERE NEW?

Police efforts to find a suspicious money trail linked to the ambush slaying of Jerzy Schroeder on his Maryland estate three weeks ago have turned up nothing useful, according to a source connected with law enforcement who spoke on condition of anonymity because public disclosure of the results has not been authorized. Another person familiar with the investigation confirmed that nothing was found.

With no results to show for weeks of painstaking police work focused on one theory about the murder, law enforcement authorities nevertheless declined to confirm hints that the focus of their efforts has shifted.

"We have never limited the investigation to any one person of interest," Maryland State Police spokesperson Melissa Dallywahl said by e-mail yesterday. "Or of potential interest. We have identified a number of possibly fruitful lines of inquiry and, with

the cooperation of the D.C. Metropolitan
Police and other law enforcement agencies,
we will continue to pursue them. We have not
ruled out any theory; nor have we identified
any possibility that we intend to examine to
the exclusion of other possible explanations
for this extremely serious crime."

Experienced observers of procedures
usually followed by metro-area police
agencies investigating major crimes point
out that it is in fact common for police to
focus on what they view as the most likely
suspect and solution as soon as they have
identified one. Several independent sources
confirmed that Maryland police indeed appear
to have done that in this case, theorizing
that Schroeder was murdered out of jealousy
as the result of an adulterous affair. They
appear to have been unable to develop solid
evidence to support that theory, however,
and there are now strong indications that
they have begun to look actively at another
possibility, involving a different suspect
and a different motive. To some observers,
Ms. Dallywahl's reference to "a number of
possibly fruitful lines of inquiry" suggested
oblique confirmation of that inference.

I had to admire the nimble way Terry had tiptoed through
the defamation minefield. He hadn't identified Rafe as the
suspected homicidally jealous husband or me as Jerzy's *objet
d'amour*. Anyone who'd been following the story would get the
hint, but that wasn't Terry's fault, was it?

I also liked "experienced observers," which meant Terry and
another reporter he has lunch with. That's an old-school way for
reporters to put their own background knowledge into a story
without just coming out and saying so.

So it seemed like the story should really pep me up. Looked
like Rafe was off the hook, with the spotlight on someone else:
Dierdorf, presumably, but maybe Klimchock or even DeHoic,

for all I knew. Didn't matter to me, as long as it wasn't Rafe. If "other law enforcement agencies" meant the FBI—and it sure as Hell didn't mean the National Park Police, did it?—then it looked like Jerzy the gangster rather than Jerzy the lover was the one who'd caught a bullet.

Somehow, though, I just couldn't feel good about the thing. Something in it tied a nasty knot of anxiety in my belly—almost enough to make me lose my taste for the martini waiting for me at home.

Almost.

Damage Control Strategy, Day 23

(the fourth Friday after the murder)

Chapter Forty-three

"Love the script," the voice over the speaker in Seamus' office said Friday morning. "Love the vocals. Just love 'em."

I closed my eyes, balled my fists, and gritted my teeth. Waiting for 'but.'

"Great," Seamus said in a wary voice—wary because he also figured 'but' was coming.

"But we wonder if maybe we could, you know, punch up the visuals just a bit."

"We?" As Seamus spoke that word I had no trouble imagining the rage flaring inside his glass head.

"I mean you, of course, on our nickel. We wouldn't ask you to keep working on spec."

"How many nickels?"

"Let's say ten thousand just to cover your costs on this visual punch-up. Dollars. Ten thousand dollars. Not ten thousand nickels."

The disembodied voice chuckled in a way that made me think of a found-footage horror movie. I got real focused real fast. For ten thousand dollars up front, Seamus would agree to any visual punch-up short of full frontal nudity—and I'm not completely sure he would have balked at that.

"What do you have in mind?" Seamus asked.

"Well, do you think you could see your way clear to shooting the thing one more time, just the way you did it, everything the same—except this time, at a place near Chambersburg, Pennsylvania, called Sportsman's and Shooter's Supply?"

"Yes."

"This afternoon?"

"Yes, uh, I mean, if we can get the videographer on short notice."

"Don't worry about the videographer. We'll provide one. You just have your pretty little lady with her snub-nose and her attitude there at, say, two o'clock. How about that?"

"You got it." Seamus glanced at his watch and gulped.

"Good. Real good."

All of a sudden I didn't need to worry about having any time on my hands on Friday. Took us most of the morning and early afternoon to get there. Found a huge, ramshackle wooden building, as if someone had taken a Western town street-front from a Hollywood set for a cowboy movie, except with actual walls and rooms behind the façade, and set it in the middle of a parking lot for a 1950s drive-in theater. A boardwalk shaded by an overhang must have stretched a good two hundred feet along the storefront, with dozens of people strolling along it. Two men and women in Amish dress had lifted a beautifully joined oak gun cabinet onto the boardwalk, presumably so that they could try to sell a line of the things to the store's proprietor when he got a chance to look at it.

Guy named Caleb Early was waiting for us. Big, bushy beard, homespun jeans and shirt, warm smile, and nestled in an open holster strapped to his right hip—something Wyatt Earp might have carried. He walked us to a shooting gallery in the back, taking us past so many guns and rifles that it seemed like every soldier in the Iraqi Army could have dropped one while running away and there'd still have been plenty left. Sleek, squeaky clean, and well-lighted, the gallery looked big enough to accommodate an entire class of FBI trainees.

The videographer had already set up a tripod-mounted camera that you could have used to film a made-for-TV rom-com. Her name was Cat. Just Cat, no last name. Cat the videographer. Said so right there on her card. The baseball cap she wore and the equipment bag she carried both had NRA logos on them. If she was constitutionally carrying, at least she had the weapon out of sight.

The human outline target this time had white lines on a black background rather than the other way around. Hmm… And the bull's-eye target heart looked like it was about the size of a dinner plate.

Two rehearsals, then we started shooting. Finally got through it on the fourth try. Even using a snub-nose—much less accurate than a gun with four-inch barrel, like the one Jerzy and I had plinked with—six holes, three fairly high in the torso, one actually in the heart. Seamus examined the target critically.

"Maybe we should go one more time and see if we can get at least four bullets in the heart-lung area," he said. "For, you know, optics."

"Don't worry your pretty little head about it," Cat said distractedly. "By dinnertime tonight this little movie will show six shots in the kill-zone. I only shoot with a camera, but I *never* miss." She unbolted the camera from the tripod and hoisted it to her right shoulder. "Let's go up front and get a shot of Josie paying for the ammunition and gallery time. For, you know, optics."

"Sure." Seamus nodded and nudged me with his left elbow, meaning, I hoped, that MVC would reimburse me.

Simple enough. Putting a twenty and a five next to a cash register and collecting change, a cartridge box, and a receipt didn't really call for a lot of method acting chops. Managed to get it done without hamming it up.

Finished. Finally. Not real comfortable with the whole thing. Didn't like the movie magic and the professional slickness. I mean, for Heaven sakes, I couldn't qualify for the Olympic pistol team but I can do enough damage to a target thirty feet away to take him out of the fight. *Really* didn't like the black target. Most of all, I didn't like the feeling that this thing was now completely out of my control, and Seamus', and MVC's.

But at least it was over. Two to three hours and close to a

hundred miles from here Rafe and a cocktail were waiting for me. I could already smell the gin.

Out of habit, I looked at the receipt, not printed out from a computer under the cash register but handwritten on a carbon pad form, as if 1972 were thinking about a comeback.

SPORTSMAN'S AND SHOOTER'S SUPPLY
Chambersburg, Pennsylvania
"The Very Best in Sporting Arms and Self-Defense"
NRA Sustaining Member

Merchandise	$ 7.95
Services	16.50
LCD (10%)	(2.45)
Subtotal:	$ 22.00
Pa. State Sales Tax @ 6%	1.32
Total:	$ 23.32

LCD? Huh? Had I bought a large-screen TV without realizing it? 'Cause good luck getting reimbursed for that from Seamus.

"What's LCD?" I asked.

"Loyal Customer Discount, Ms. Kendall." Caleb nodded earnestly. "Family plan. Your husband was in here a couple of times maybe a month, six weeks ago. He didn't use his name; guess he didn't want any special favors. I recognized him because one of his authors and I had book signings at the same store in Fredericksburg when my last book came out. *Stalking the Elusive White Tail: Deer Hunting in Deep Winter*. He was real nice, courteous and all, even though I wasn't in anything like the same class as his author, fame-wise or any other wise. Anyway, this is your family's third visit to the store, so you qualify for the Loyal Customer Discount."

"Why, thank you! Thank you so much! That is just so nice of you!"

Before those words were all the way out of my mouth, I noticed a display shelf on the wall behind the cash-register counter. Yellow rectangular boxes said "Weaver Four Power

Scopes." Yellow square boxes said, "Weaver Scope Mounting Rings." Whatever Rafe had bought here, the receipt would presumably say "merchandise" and "services," as mine did—not "telescopic sight," "mounting rings," and "x hours of target practice in the shooting gallery." And it wouldn't have Rafe's name on it anyway. Seamus would explain to me later that a lot of firearms dealers keep their descriptions generic if they legally can, because half their customers think federal agents might drop by at any moment to check on what caliber of bullets the customers were buying. So no cops would find any smoking-gun paper trail here, even if they happened to look. Still…

Now I understood what had bothered me about Terry Fielding's article yesterday. The investigation wasn't really over for Rafe. It didn't make any difference what we did, how much we cooperated, how many trails turned into dead ends. Until the cops had actually nailed someone else, any little thing—like a chance memory of Rafe coming to an out-of-the-way gun shop not too long before Jerzy bought the farm—could bring him right back to center stage under a full spotlight.

Not that they could make anything out of it, as far as I could see. They couldn't shake the Theo McAbbott alibi without a money trail, and there wasn't a money trail. QED, as Sister Yvette taught me to write after I'd finished a proof in geometry. *Quod erat demonstrandum*, which is Latin for something or other that boils down to *I rest my case*. But still, they'd want him to explain why he'd come here, and why he hadn't mentioned it before, and isn't it a funny coincidence, and all that stuff. Open up a whole new can of worms, and it would just never be over.

I started to feel a little sorry for myself. Shook that off fast. No poor-little-me. I'd made this mess. I didn't see how I could clean it up without getting on the shit-lists of some badass folks, but at least I could keep from making it worse.

Chapter Forty-four

It was a tough way to end the week. Doubts. I'm not much for doubts, but about halfway through my Friday night martini I realized I had one now.

Not about Rafe. I'd thought the whole thing through again on the drive back. Same answers as before. The queasy uncertainty I felt fluttering in my gut was about me. Did I actually have a chokepoint after all? Seriously? Josie? Chokepoint? Were there things—perfectly legal things—that I couldn't bring myself to do to win a political fight?

Twenty-four hours ago I would've bet everything I had on no. Clips of John Kerry zig-zagging on a sailboard to hammer home the idea that he'd flip-flopped on Iraq? No problem. Senator Harry Reid's false "rumor" that Mitt Romney hadn't paid any taxes in ten years? Politics ain't touch football. Bill Clinton pulling the white backlash ploy in South Carolina when Hillary headed downhill against Obama in 2008? If you can do identity politics, I can do identity politics. The 1964 "daisy ad" with a voiceover countdown to a mushroom cloud appearing behind a little girl to make the point that Barry Goldwater would start a nuclear war? That's the way the game is played. You do politics with me, you'd best come with your ankles taped.

All of a sudden, though, I caught myself banging up against an invisible limit, like a family dog penned in by an electronic fence. I think Rafe spotted it right away, but he gave me space to work it out for myself. I finally opened up to him just before bed.

"I can't do it, honey. I just can't do it."

"The concealed carry campaign?"

"*Constitutional* carry. I mean, yes. I can handle the concept. Using that black target, though—that's just too much. The target doesn't have to be black to make the point. They're just using a black target to appeal to subliminal, racist fears that a lot of people have without even knowing it. Vestigial terror of black men, of the savage black thug, barely human, lurking in alleys and hijacking cars and breaking into homes. I just can't swallow it. Especially after all that's happened in the last couple of years, I just can't."

"For someone whose mind is supposed to be fast but not deep, that's pretty profound."

"I don't feel like you have to get much below the surface to spot this issue. Given what the country has gone through from Trayvon Martin on, and especially the black community. People see a twenty-two-year-old black male in a hoodie walking down the sidewalk toward them thirty feet away and their hands automatically move toward their guns? Dear God, I just can't be part of reinforcing that. Exploiting that. Playing to that."

Rafe didn't say another word at first. He just sat there next to me on the couch, gazing at me with tender thoughtfulness. He let the silence hang between us for a good ten seconds. Then he spoke to me in a soft, coaxing tone like you might use with a teenager who's just been dumped for the first time.

"I have never been prouder of you than I am at this moment. I have never been more thrilled to be your husband."

Those words jazzed me up more than a call from the White House operator asking me to hold for the chief of staff would have. I started to tear up, then just collapsed against him so that he could hold me to his chest.

"You'll decide for yourself what you have to do about this, Josie. It won't be easy, but I can tell you one thing. You can trust yourself to get to the right answer—and when you do, you'll be absolutely sure about it. Not happy, necessarily, but absolutely sure."

Damage Control Strategy, Day 26

(the fourth Monday after the murder)

Damage Control Strategy,
Day 26

(the fourth Monday after the murder)

Chapter Forty-five

I woke up Monday morning with the most wonderful feeling. Not just calm. Serene. Free of doubt. I knew just what I was going to do, and I knew I was right.

As Rafe had said, that didn't make it easy. Good jobs are scarce in D.C. these days, and I was about to throw one away. Not only that, but I'd be giving everyone in town a good reason to think three or four times before offering me another one.

I made it to MVC early so that I could get settled and swallow some coffee before telling Seamus that I couldn't do the constitutional carry campaign unless we dropped the racial subtext. Squared my shoulders in front of MVC's suite as I got my key-card ready to scan the lock open. I reminded myself that I might be using that key-card for the very last time. Took a deep breath. *Maybe while I'm between jobs I can write a book on conservative fund-raising: "The Joy of Koching."*

I scanned the card. *Please let Seamus be in a decent mood when he comes in.* Heard the *thunk* of the lock opening, which brought back tummy-tumbling memories of its own. Opened the door. And heard Seamus' outraged screams bouncing off every wall in the entire suite.

"Those *bastards*! Those sniveling little *weasels*! Those pencil-pushing, anal-obsessive, heads-up-their-butts, desk-jockey *bureaucrats*! How could they *do* this? How could even they possibly sink so low? It's obscene! How could they do it?"

Indictment? Audit notice? Civil investigative demand from the Federal Elections Commission? IRS lien? Revocation of our tax-exempt status?

I scurried toward his office. Found him standing purple-faced behind his desk, raking the fingers of his right hand through his hair while he stared in furious dudgeon at two stapled pages held in his left. He noticed me.

"What is this?" he demanded indignantly. "What is this thing?"

He sounded as if he really wanted to know. Three quick strides brought me close enough to pluck the packet from his quivering fingers.

"Well, for one thing," I said, "it's addressed to me."

"Yeah." Seamus shrugged at that detail. "It came in with Saturday's mail. I found it when I got in early this morning, and figured I'd better take a look at it."

"Oh. Well, I guess I'd better take a look at it too." I did.

> Dear Ms. Kendall:
>
> I am pleased to inform you that your application for a permit to carry the firearm specified on the enclosed license within the territorial boundaries of the District of Columbia has been approved. You should have the license on your person *at all times* when you are in possession of the firearm within the District.
>
> Please note that this license does *not* make it legal for you to carry this or any other firearm in any jurisdiction other than the District of Columbia. Before taking the weapon outside the District, you should familiarize yourself with the laws and licensing requirements in any jurisdiction in which you will be traveling.
>
> Please note that IT IS YOUR RESPONSIBILITY as a gun-owner to be familiar with ALL applicable legal provisions relating to the safe and lawful use of firearms. *Some* applicable District of Columbia ordinances may be found on the website referenced on the enclosed license. THIS COMPILATION IS

NOT EXHAUSTIVE. You are advised to consult counsel of your own choice about other obligations you may have.

I dropped the letter disconsolately on Seamus' desk and slapped on an expression suggesting that my dog had just died. Obviously, it wouldn't do to give Seamus a hint of the toga party going on inside my head at the moment.

"This ruins everything, doesn't it?" I moaned.

"Well, it sure doesn't help."

Seamus collapsed theatrically in his chair. The chair arched to the limit of its springs as Seamus thrust his head and body back in frustrated despair.

"You know what, though?" I said perkily. "This isn't the end of the world."

"No. At the end of the world angels will be riding around on red and green horses killing people one-hundred-forty-four-thousand at a time or something. But this is pretty damn close."

"Maybe. You might be absolutely right. But there just might be a way we could retrieve this situation."

"How?" Seamus gave me a wary, wide-eyed look.

"We own the concept and the visuals, right?"

"I suppose. But so what?"

"The permit proves that our concept works. A little web-heat and the regulators fold. Now all we need to do is find another Josie Kendall in some city that's tight-assed about concealed carry. We can replicate the campaign with her."

Seamus brightened. Well, not so much 'brightened' exactly. More looked like he'd moved up from suicidal to clinically depressed.

"Maybe…" He sounded like his heart wasn't in it.

"And you know what? Make her an African-American. Can't use the black target then, but that's a detail."

"No!" Seamus leaped to his feet so fast that I jumped back, startled. "Not *an* African-American woman! An African-American woman, a Caucasian woman, a Hispanic woman, and an

Asian woman! A rainbow coalition for Second Amendment rights! God, this could be huge!"

"But no black target. Can't mix the message."

"Absolutely right. Right, right, right. No mixed messages!" Seamus clapped his hands and rubbed his palms together with unbecoming relish. I beamed at him.

"You're a genius, Boss."

"That's true." He shrugged. "But you bring out the best in me."

Damage Control Strategy, Day 28

(the fourth Wednesday after the murder)

Chapter Forty-six

Wednesday, 10:23 a.m. That's when it happened.

I still had both a job and a clear conscience. Seamus was busily lashing the excellent nerds into pursuit of four markswomen diverse enough for a Benetton ad. The Rafe-and-Josie damage control plan had basically worked. I sat there at my desk, slogging away at the America-back-into-space thing while CNN Breaking News streamed silently on my iPad. As long as the heat was off Rafe, no need for me to make a bigger blip on the killer's radar screen than I already had. Still lots of unanswered questions, but I wasn't going to do a blessed thing to answer them unless something just fell in my lap.

At 10:23 something fell in my lap.

My phone rang at 10:19. Ann DeHoic's number showed up on the caller ID screen. I held off through the second ring, then instinct took over and I answered. DeHoic, as usual, got right to the point.

"I need you to sign off on the plea deal on the burglary. You're too smart to ask why I want his case resolved, so don't."

I glared at the phone. *You have a talent for pissing me off, girl.* Thought that, but didn't say it. I said something else instead.

"The 'why' question I had in mind was why I should do you any favors."

"Because I can do something for you that no one else can."

"All ears, *chica.*"

Exasperated sigh from DeHoic. Couldn't blame her. She got over it.

"Jerzy was killed while you and he were on your way to meet a potential investor in the wind power thing, right?"

"Yes."

"Jerzy had emailed the investor to confirm the time and place of the meeting."

"That doesn't come as a complete surprise."

"The server he used to store those e-mails was hacked the day before the meeting—about four hours before Dierdorf told his pilot to be ready to fly to D.C. first thing next morning."

"I see."

"I'll just bet you do," DeHoic said. "The server should have electronic markers showing the fact, date, and timing of the hack. The computer used to infiltrate Jerzy's server figures to have Dierdorf's fingerprints all over it. Figuratively speaking, but even so. Not enough to put him in the electric chair, because Maryland doesn't have the balls to execute murderers these days, but combined with everything else, it should make him the only plausible suspect—which is all you care about."

"True." All of a sudden I wasn't feeling so sassy. "The police must already have the server, so all I have to do is tell them what to look for and convince them to spend the time and effort required to find it."

"Not that simple." DeHoic favored me with her second sigh of the conversation. "The police don't have the server. It's still at his house."

"I'm betting you can tell me where to find it." I had to work at keeping my tone civil, but I managed it.

"I can help you find it. Just as important, I can get you into the house so you can look for it."

"In exchange for my helping this incompetent thug who has a grudge against me get off with a wrist slap."

"Pretty much."

Well I'll tell you what, Ms. DeHoic. You go right straight to Hell and don't stop for coffee on the way. I am officially off the Sanford

Dierdorf posse. I had that answer right on the tip of my tongue. At 10:23, though, just before I would have slammed the door in DeHoic's face, something on the CNN feed caught my eye. Couldn't say why, at first, but it tripped a synapse or two that started eight cylinders revving in that fast-but-not-deep brain of mine. I figured I'd better stall DeHoic while I tried to figure out what the trigger was.

"Just out of curiosity, how can you get me into the house?"

"I'm the executrix of his estate. Strike that. Executor. Executrix is sexist."

While she ran through that jazz I clicked back to the CNN home page and found the link to the story I'd been streaming: "Pres Leaves for Camp David Amid Cong. Debate Over Treaty." I went back to DeHoic long enough to keep the ball in the air with her.

"Still executor years after you divorced? How does that work?"

She launched into a riff about love is love but money is money, except with a lot more words than that. I didn't pay much attention, focusing instead on clicking the Leaves-for-Camp-David story and watching it replay. The visuals looked like stuff I'd seen a hundred times. Almost stock footage. The President and First Lady walking across the White House south lawn toward the helicopter dubbed *Marine One*, trailed by a quartet of close aides. The camera followed the group as the helicopter rotor and fuselage came into the shot. *Okay. So what?*

Then, all it once, it just leaped out at me. Aide number two—Gerri Chapman. Rafe and I were on a first-name basis with her. She had a book pinned between her right hand and her envelope-style briefcase. Not the way you'd normally carry a book. Awkwardly but carefully positioned so that every reporter on the south lawn—including the one behind CNN's camera—could see the cover and read the title: *Ducks in a Row*, by Theo McAbbott.

Everything dropped into place. Why Jerzy had recruited me by dangling a million-dollar campaign in front of me; what my real role was supposed to be; how Dierdorf's handgun had ended up in Jerzy's possession; which actors I could trust and which ones might try to kill me if I didn't watch my step closer than a hanging chad; and (most important) who had killed Jerzy and why.

DeHoic's well-rehearsed explanation hadn't yet run its course. I cut in.

"All right, Ms. DeHoic, we've got a deal. I'll tell my lawyer to sign off on the Reuter plea arrangement as soon as I have that server in my hands."

"When can we get together at Jerzy's house?"

"Let me check my To-Do list." I glanced at a blank sheet on top of a legal pad next to my iPad. "How about Friday afternoon?"

"Done. We can meet outside the main entrance to Annapolis Mall on the outskirts of Annapolis at one and drive over together."

As soon as DeHoic had hung up, I picked up a ballpoint and attacked the pad:

TO DO:

1. Call Mama.

Chapter Forty-seven

For my Mama-chat I closed my office door and used the cell phone that Seamus doesn't know about. I laid it all out for her, except for the part that she, and especially Uncle Darius, were better off not knowing. You know, plausible deniability. She listened in her no-judgments/no-nonsense way, just as she had during talks about whether I should be on the pill, my short-lived exploration of marijuana, and what Carondelet primly called my occasional "deportment issues." Concern in her voice, but no panic, once I'd finished and she spoke up.

"Well, from the looks of things, Josie, you're in a heap of trouble."

"Yes, Mama."

"Do you have a plan?"

"Sure do."

"Shoot."

"Shooting is only part of it." I explained my plan, including the element that would include literally shooting.

"High risk, high reward." A tincture of approval colored Mama's voice—a good thing, because I was sure in the mood for some. "But I wonder if I might make a suggestion?"

"Of course you can, Mama."

"'May.'"

"Sorry. Of course you may, Mama."

"I think your uncle might play a constructive role in this."

Pulling the phone from my ear, I flat out gaped at it. I don't think I'd ever heard anyone, let alone Mama, use 'constructive' in a sentence about Uncle Darius.

"Mama, the last time I involved Uncle D in this mess, he got himself all banged up."

"Which was his own blessed fault. But in the process he came up with some real useful information for you."

"This is true," I admitted. "And I'm the first one to say he could be helpful again. But if you draw a circle around the Washington, D.C. metropolitan area, including the Maryland and northern Virginia suburbs and exurbs, he would have to be useful from at least seven-thousand feet outside that circle, because according to some NRA folks I've talked to in the last week or so, six-thousand-five-hundred feet is the maximum effective range for a non-military grade firearm."

"What I have in mind is him being effective from Baton Rouge, Louisiana—and I'll be standing at the door with a baseball bat to brain him with, in case he tries to skedaddle before you're done."

"Mama, that sounds very promising."

After Mama and I had finished talking, I revised the list in front of me:

TO DO BEFORE FRIDAY

√ 1. Talk to Mama.
2. Talk to Tony.
3. Talk to Klimchock.
4. Visit Shooter's Paradise. Bring cash.

Good start. Tony and I were talking fifteen seconds after I'd dialed his number.

"Is this about Reuter?"

"Yep. You'll get either an e-mail or a phone call from me Friday afternoon saying that I'm okay with the plea deal. Ignore it unless it includes the words '*pas de merde.*'"

I'd halfway expected some push-back on that. Didn't happen.

"Got it," Tony said. Then, being a lawyer, he spelled out *pas de merde*. Got it right, too.

Klimchock was a tougher nut to crack. When we'd talked at Dulles he'd said he'd be overseas for a week, which meant he should have gotten back by now. I called all three numbers on the business card he'd given me, though, plus the different number I got for him from my phone's Recent Calls list, but I had to leave four voicemails. I asked him to use a land-line when he returned my call, and to call my desk-phone number at work. By the time I left for Shooter's Paradise, he still hadn't gotten back to me.

I did Shooter's Paradise during the afternoon, because I didn't want to make up a story for Rafe about why I was unexpectedly going out after dinner. I toted my certifiably legal Colt snub-nose to the shooting gallery in back and fired six shots at one of the human outline targets. I'm pretty sure I hit with all six, but I didn't really pay that much attention.

Klimchock finally returned my call at six-fifteen, after I'd gotten back to the office from Shooter's Paradise and was cleaning up some things before going home for the day.

"Can I interest you in some applied engineering solutions involving hydraulics or thermodynamics, Ms. Kendall, or is something else on your mind?"

"Okay, this is going to sound a little, uh, *elliptical*."

"You're talking to me from Washington, so that would figure."

"Here's the deal. I have no reason to believe that you could get in touch with Sanford Dierdorf, or with anyone who could get a message to him. And I have no reason to believe that you care one way or another what happens to him. But I do have reason to believe that he has received word in the last twenty-four hours suggesting that he visit Jerzy Schroeder's former Maryland residence this Friday. If, by some wild chance you *could* get in touch with him, and if for some reason you might wish to do him a favor, you might tell him that it would be a good idea for him to RSVP with regrets."

"Because why?"

"Because he will be walking into a trap."

"I take it," Klimchock said after five or six intriguing seconds, "that as a law-abiding person you would not ask me to warn Mr. Dierdorf away from a meeting where the FBI is planning to arrest him."

"You are correct. I wouldn't do that. My felony quota for this fiscal year is zero, and obstruction of justice would put me over it."

"Me too. Message received. Jesus loves you and wants you to be saved. No further comment."

"Got it. You have a real good day, now."

The closer we got to Friday, the more tension roiled my gut and the more excitement I felt tingling through my body. Fear, too, of course. I was scared, for sure, but it was a good scared—the kind you get before a volleyball match against a strong team with a reputation for hard spikes aimed at your face.

The hardest part was, I couldn't talk to Rafe about any of it. The key things I just couldn't tell him. Yet.

Damage Control Strategy, Day 30

(the fifth Friday after the murder)

Damage Control Strategy
Day 30

(the fifth Friday after the murder)

Chapter Forty-eight

I waltzed into the Annapolis Mall's main entrance at straight up noon on Friday. An hour early, on purpose. I planted myself in a rear corner of the modest entryway between the huge, glass outside doors and the not quite as huge glass doors opening into the abundantly air-conditioned mall itself. I had a decent view of a designated smoking area well outside, on the opposite end of the entrance. I'm not trying to pass myself off as Sherlock Holmes or anything, but it didn't exactly shock me to the soles of my feet when DeHoic showed up there at twelve-thirty-five.

She did the silver case and Piaget lighter thing, igniting her cigarette with an elegant aplomb truly impressive for someone wearing a gray pantsuit in ninety-three-degree heat. I let her get in three calming puffs as she impatiently surveyed the patrons traipsing toward the entrance from the parking lot. Then I went out and approached her.

"Good afternoon."

"You're early," she said, giving me a startled look.

"That's the way I was brought up: early for appointments, late for parties, right on time for supper."

"Did you bring that belly-gun you've been campaigning for on the Internet?"

"Like the Coast Guard says, *Semper paratus*. Always ready."

"All right, then." She put her cigarette through an inconspicuous hole in a waist-high tube that seemed to have been deliberately designed to look like it had nothing to do with smoking. "My car is right over there. Let's go."

"You know what? Let's take my car instead." I started strolling toward my Fusion. "It'll be harder to follow. A myopic cyclops could keep that Mercedes of yours in sight even on the freeway, much less on country roads."

"You expect us to be followed?"

"Hope for the best, plan for the worst." I half-shouted this over my shoulder, because I was moving steadily forward while DeHoic hesitated.

She still hadn't moved when I clicked my Fusion open and climbed in. We had a good two hundred feet between us by now. Pulling out of my parking space with a little tire-squeal, I wheeled around three rows of parked cars and pulled up to the curb with the passenger-side door toward DeHoic.

"Climb on in. You can smoke in here if you want to. Won't bother me."

That closed the sale. She folded herself into the seat and slammed the door, just in case I didn't know she was pissed off. Out came her cell phone.

"I'll tell my driver to follow us."

"That would defeat the purpose. Tell him to meet us there if you want to, but make sure he stays at least a mile behind us."

By now I'd gotten us out of the parking lot and onto a four-lane road with a forty-mile-per-hour speed limit that drivers seemed to regard as just a friendly suggestion.

"Are you serious about this cops-and-robbers stuff?" she demanded.

I'd been waiting for that one. With my right hand I opened the purse in my lap and took out the snub-nose. Thumbing back a knurled knob on the left side of the gun's frame, just behind the cylinder, I used two fingers on the right side to push the cylinder out. I held it up with the breech in DeHoic's general direction so that she could see the brass bases of six cartridge casings. Not just showing her the gun—after all, I'd already told her I had it—but showing her I could handle the thing proficiently without any help from Photoshop.

"That's how serious I am, sister." I snapped the cylinder back into place with a determined wrist-flick and re-stowed the Colt in my purse. "After I got Jerzy's brains splattered all over my blouse, several people told me, indirectly, that Sanford Dierdorf is the one who put them there. One of those people was you. Now you've promised to hand me evidence that will hang the sonofabitch, figuratively speaking—so don't act like we're on our way to a tea party."

That pretty much stopped the conversation. She seemed a little nervous. She looked around a couple of times, craning her neck toward the rear window, once we reached the county road intersecting the lane that ran past Jerzy's house. No idea what she saw, if anything. Plenty of cars behind us, of course. Hell's bells, this is *Maryland.* If you want privacy on a public road, go drive in Montana. Even so, I started to get a touch of the shakes myself. Power of suggestion, maybe.

We reached Jerzy's house a little after one-thirty. I parked at the east end of the driveway, behind the hedge, same as I had the day Jerzy died. DeHoic produced a key as we approached the front door. Stepping nimbly over sagging, plastic yellow crime-scene tape, we walked in like we owned the place. She didn't relock the door. Hmm...Memories radiated from the Currier and Ives prints and the oversized pastoral landscapes on the faded red living room walls, from the well-trodden ecru carpeting on the deep maple stairs, and of course from the locked cabinet built into the corner bookcase. Warm memories and sinister memories and shaming memories. I choked them back as DeHoic led me up to the master bedroom, on the southwest corner of the second floor.

It looked a lot like it had the last time I'd left it, roughly ten minutes before Jerzy's head exploded. The bed, with its head against the center of the west wall and framed by mullioned windows, still looked big enough for a three-way and then some. Satin sheets rumpled, pillows thrown every which way at the head, royal blue combed cotton duvet bunched down at the foot, remnants of the *Times* and the *Post* scattered here and there. Between the northwest corner and a bathroom door stood a man's chest of drawers, with the drawers all slightly open, presumably the way the crime-scene team had left them. Blank space on the floor at the opposite end of the north wall, where DeHoic's dresser and vanity presumably had sat before the break-up. Interesting homey touch that she'd taken them. In the corner near the chest sat a straight-back chair draped with a tux Jerzy presumably had worn the night before he died. Patent leather dress shoes rested almost fastidiously on the floor underneath the chair.

A semi-circle of sweat beaded across the back of DeHoic's neck as she went to the windows on the south wall. No air-conditioning in the house now, of course, but I chalked the sweat up to more than Washington's high-summer heat. This was no longer the icy-cool, disdainful DeHoic that I'd gotten to know. Standing to one side of the windows, she nudged the filmy drape a few inches away from her with her right hand. She gazed toward the road for a good ten seconds. Same routine then with the windows on the west side.

"Is there something you should be sharing with me?" I asked.

"I'm not sure the car-switch you insisted on accomplished much. I had the feeling someone *was* following us on our way out here."

"If you're trying to get me good and scared, you've managed it nicely. So let's just find the server you promised me and get out of here as fast as we can."

DeHoic went down on her knees near the foot of the bed on the side near her. She reached underneath the frame, and started fiddling with something on the inside. She'd been at it for five or six seconds, with no results that I could see, when a distinct, metal-on-metal *snap* sounded from downstairs.

Chapter Forty-nine

DeHoic looked up at me, her expression mildly annoyed rather than scared or startled. My assumption that she expected Dierdorf to join the party was starting to look pretty good.

"That's probably nothing," she muttered. "Old houses come with odd, random noises. But humor me, okay? Stand over there near the window on this side of the bed, facing the door, and get that Junior G-Woman cap gun of yours ready."

I thought about it. I'd put the chances of company at no better than one in five. Sure, maybe Klimchock hadn't contacted Dierdorf, or maybe Dierdorf hadn't listened to him, but Dierdorf figured to see DeHoic's invitation as a low-percentage play, in any event. When you hear a dubious noise split the still summer air in an almost empty house, though, probability calculations get a second look.

I crossed the room. Didn't stand in front of the window, of course. Got my back against the wall in a space between the west-side windows and the corner. Unholstered my Colt. And without making a production out of it, took out my cell phone, punched a speed-dial number, and as I set the phone on the sill prayed that Mama would keep Uncle D's mouth shut when they accepted the call.

DeHoic went back to fingering the inside of the bed's long, solid side brace. A tiny, whispering, almost apologetic *thok* sounded from under the bed. As a small, hidden drawer slid smoothly out from the frame, *creak* came from the stairway—the main staircase, which you'd use if you came in the front door; not the back stair case that Jerzy and I had used the last time he'd used anything.

DeHoic took a thumb-drive out of the drawer and held it up so that I could see it. Not a server. Hmm... *What if there's a gun in that drawer, too?* For two terrible seconds I wondered if I'd blown the whole thing through sheer carelessness, but DeHoic stood up holding the thumb-drive and nothing else.

"It's all on here."

Another *creak*, this one from the top of the stairs.

"Get ready with that gun!" she stage-whispered at me. Fierce but calm.

I kept the Colt held lightly in my right hand, along my right thigh. Cocked it because, really, why not? The edge of the bedroom door pushed maybe three inches into the room. Then it stopped. I held my breath.

"Steady," she muttered, still under her breath, going for calm and reassuring and sounding wound-tight tense instead. "Ready...ready..."

Nothing happened. I stayed the way I was. The door didn't move another millimeter. No sound that I could hear from outside it. My gut tightened and every muscle in my body tingled. My nerves were screaming *Do SOMETHING! ANYTHING!*—and I had actually foreseen this and thought it through. I could only imagine what games DeHoic's neurons were playing with her.

"You can come on in if you want to, Dierdorf," she called. "We're all friends here."

The door crashed open, banging loudly against the bedroom wall. After a breathtaking two seconds, a large male figure filled the doorway for an eyeblink.

"Look out!" DeHoic shouted. "Gun! Shoot!"

Was she warning me, or telling Dierdorf that *I* had a gun and he should shoot *me*? I figured she wanted to have it both ways. It only took the entrant about a quarter-second to hit the deck, scurry along the floor toward the opposite side of the bed, and then roll toward the bathroom door next to the chest. I got just the barest glimpse of him—but that was enough to know how to play the rest of my hand.

"Negative on the shooting thing," I said.

"You fucking wimp! Give me that!"

Throwing down the thumb-drive, DeHoic leaped across the room at me and grabbed the Colt, snatching it from my hands without much of an argument from me. The intruder was still prudently hugging the floor with everything but his right arm, which was reaching toward the bathroom doorknob. About a third of his body was visible from our side of the bed. DeHoic aimed my Colt at it. She squeezed the trigger.

Snap-CLICK. No gunshot. Baffled, DeHoic squeezed it again and again. Same result: *Snap-CLICK!* every time.

Our guest had now gotten the bathroom door open. After the fourth *CLICK*, though, he yelped at us instead of diving through the opening.

"Hey! What the Hell!" Klimchock's voice.

"Don't take it personally," I called. "She thought you were Dierdorf. Feel free to join the party. No one is going to be shooting anyone."

Klimchock came gingerly to a squat, facing us over the bed. DeHoic, still holding the gun, backed toward the head of the bed and flicked confused and wary eyes from me to him.

"Ms. DeHoic," I said, "I am pleased to introduce Daniel Klimchock, an applications engineer. I'm surprised you haven't met before, as he is a former associate of your late ex-husband. Mr. Klimchock, this is Ann DeHoic, known to the tabloids as 'the gray lady.' I hope you'll forgive her if she seems a bit jumpy today."

"Seriously?" Klimchock said. "A revolver made by Colt Firearms Company serially misfired?"

"Oh, it fired those bullets just fine last night. I left the cartridge shells in the cylinder after I fired them, though, so just now that firing pin was only hitting empty brass. Figured if it got fired today it would most likely be by someone else."

"Oh." Klimchock shook his head from side to side as he stood up. "Well, I guess that explains that, then. What about the computer thing?"

"That's the thumb-drive lying on the floor over there."

"Don't move!" DeHoic said, still holding the Colt with both hands and looking a bit wildly from me to Klimchock and back.

"Who you kidding, honey?" I demanded. "That gun ain't worth spit when it's not loaded. Why don't you just give it back to me?"

DeHoic turned a warrior-princess glare on me as a combination of loathing and contempt radiated from her eyes.

"Come and get it, you cracker bitch!"

"Now that's just plain rude." Two determined strides brought me close enough to DeHoic to feint a punch with my left fist while I got my right ready to smack some manners into her.

My last fight had come at nineteen when I'd found myself bent backwards over the beer pong table in the basement of TKE House at Tulane, fending off a frat boy who had his hopes up and his pants down. We'd gone at it pretty well, with me holding my own until the racket pulled enough sober TKEs into the room to moot any prospect of non-consensual sexual union. The frat boy had had to see Campus Medical the next day about "painful urinary discharge," so I'd called that one a win, fat lip and all.

DeHoic didn't have the frat boy's muscles but she had a lot more brains and her pants weren't down. Both hands still wrapped around the Colt, she stepped inside my right arm and smashed my nose and lips with the back of her right hand, reinforced by the weight of the gun and the strength of her left arm. I staggered backwards as stars exploded in my head and blood burst from my nose.

"Chick fight!" Klimchock yelled joyfully, moving toward the wall opposite the end of the bed. "Thank you, thank you, Jesus!"

Raising her right hand with that gun still in it, DeHoic strode forward to brain me with the thing. I managed to get my left arm up in time to block her, but when I tried to pop her with my right fist she half-blocked my arm and half grabbed it. Basically holding each other up, we must have looked to Klimchock like a couple of refugees from a remedial dancing class. With both arms tied up, I did the only thing I could think of: rocked my head back and snapped it forward as hard as I could to smack her right in the puss. I got the bridge of her nose with my forehead and her lips with my high, Creole/Cajun left cheekbone.

I heard something crack as white sheets of pure pain lanced through my brain. DeHoic screamed, tripping backward. Her grip on my right arm went slack. Loved the scream, but I wouldn't call the job more than half done yet. I raised my free right arm to clock her one. She somehow got her right arm swung around across her body fast enough to block my down-sweeping punch bone on bone, forearm on forearm. *Damn, this chick has some fight in her!* Only good thing was that the impact knocked the gun out of her hand, across the bed, and onto the floor.

I was running out of juice. Jogging nine-minute miles two or three times a week hadn't prepared me for the concentrated burst of total energy that this fight demanded. We'd only been at it maybe thirty seconds, but my legs were shaky, my arms felt like lead, and every breath I took seared my lungs.

DeHoic cocked her left arm to take another shot at my face. My first instinct was to duck and back up. Then I remembered "cracker bitch." Instead of retreating I sucked it up, moved forward, lowered my head just a bit, and took the punch just above the side of my right eye. Hurt like a bastard, but I'm hard-headed as Southern belles go and it didn't take me out. More important, it left DeHoic exposed on her left side. Gritting my teeth against the pain from my throbbing forearm, I wheeled my right fist up, around and down. I planted a high, hard one right on her left ear, all four knuckles and plenty of attitude behind them. She stumbled backward, fell across the bed—and covered up. I thought about putting a couple of punches into her ribs just to help her remember the experience, but I didn't do it. Mama thought I wasn't a bully; I wouldn't want to disappoint her.

"That's what we crackers down South call fighting, bitch."

I stepped back four paces with my guard still up, gulping air and keeping the one-and-a-half eyes I still had vision in on DeHoic. That ear-jab had rung her bell, all right. She rolled to a sitting position but she took her time about it and when she'd gotten it done the expression on her face made me think of a ten-year-old coming back from the woodshed. Uncle D jumped in at that point.

"Sounds like you won that little set-to, Josie."

"She sure did," Klimchock yelled with downright indecent enthusiasm. "TKO. Everything but the bloody towel in the middle of the ring. By the way, who's talking to me?"

"Oh, that's my uncle," I said. "Darius Zachary Taylor Barry. We're all about to have a conversation here, and I think it will be more constructive if everyone knows there's an impartial witness listening to us."

I guess that took the cake for DeHoic. She leaned way over at the waist and started throwing up. Tough to watch, but I couldn't think of anything to do about it.

Klimchock came through. He produced a mini-bottle of water from the right pocket of his blue blazer and a handkerchief from a rear pocket of his pants. He dampened the hankie liberally, brought it over to DeHoic, and started sponging off her mouth. He glanced at the top drawer of the chest while doing this. Taking the hint, I circled to the chest, found a month's supply of white cotton handkerchiefs in the top drawer, pulled out three of them, and brought them back around to Klimchock. He used them to dry DeHoic's mouth, then gave the bottle to her for a long swig. After scampering back to his post by the far wall, he looked at me.

"You said something about a conversation. This looks like a good time to start it."

Chapter Fifty

"This is bullshit," DeHoic spat.

"Now, Ms. DeHoic, I am very put out with you right now, and I am not interested in your opinions. What you need to do is keep your mouth buttoned up real tight while I tell you the way things are going to be."

That shut her up. I took a breath, glanced at Klimchock, then turned back toward DeHoic.

"You stole Dierdorf's pistol and gave it to Jerzy. You substituted an identical make and model. Dierdorf is mostly a poser when it comes to rough stuff, and that gun was more a prop for him than anything else. Because of the switch, he didn't realize you'd relieved him of his weapon."

"That's just pathetic," Klimchock muttered. "Didn't know his own gun. What a loser."

"How do I know this? Because that's by far the most likely way for Jerzy to have gotten the thing, and because you wouldn't have paid all that money for the pitch-file if you hadn't been up to your ears in Jerzy's scheme to grab Dierdorf's crony capitalism grant. Which brings us to the question that I, personally, find most interesting: Exactly what was that scheme?"

DeHoic opened her mouth, but I raised my index finger and she shut it real fast.

"Jerzy's plan had nothing to do with getting an audit started on Dierdorf's company. That was just the cover story he used when he started playing my ego like that violin of his. I was supposed to drive Jerzy in my car to a meeting with his key investor. Jerzy had the gun you'd taken from Dierdorf, but I didn't know it. Once we were well away from his estate, Jerzy was going to shoot me with Dierdorf's gun, leave me dead in my car, wipe the gun, and ditch it where the police would find it."

"A dish like you?" Klimchock demanded. "World class bad call."

"A dead body, a victim involved in making Dierdorf look bad, a murder weapon registered to Dierdorf, and a flight plan putting Dierdorf near the scene at the time of the murder. Never mind an audit. Sanford Dierdorf would either be a fugitive or held without bail, and either way he'd be out of the federal subsidy business."

"Why, that is just despicable!" Uncle Darius offered that chirp over the phone. "If I were up there, I'd be inclined to give someone some serious creasing up."

"That's why you're where you are, Uncle D. Luckily for me, Jerzy passed away about fifteen minutes before he would have terminated my career with extreme prejudice. If...someone hadn't murdered Jerzy, his plan would have worked real well."

"Someone?" DeHoic asked. "You aren't trying to pin Jerzy's murder on me, are you?"

"Do I look like Nancy Drew to you, sweetheart? Solving murders isn't my chosen vocation."

"Then what are you driving at?"

"Divorce or no divorce, you and Jerzy were still business partners. You pretended to break with him so that you could get close to Dierdorf and steal his gun. Whoever killed Jerzy, that makes you just as complicit as you can be in the plan to murder me, which is the main reason I am particularly pissed off at you."

"Oh." DeHoic shrugged. "Well, no harm, no foul. I'll buy you a new blouse."

"You were the one who hired Bart Reuter to snatch the pitch-file, knowing that Dierdorf would get the blame for it and you'd save a ton of money to boot. That's why you were so hot to get Reuter off the hook, before the FBI could flip him. More important, you decided not to give up on Jerzy's subsidy-snatch plan. You knew Dierdorf was worried about me because it looked like I'd been working hand-in-glove with Jerzy."

"So *that's* why that punk came after me in Denver," Uncle D said.

"Right. Then Ms. DeHoic here told Dierdorf that she could get him together with me here to work out a deal. She figured that maybe I'd shoot him or maybe he'd shoot me or, in a pinch, maybe she'd shoot both of us, but any of those outcomes would set up a subsidy-switch even better than Jerzy's original plan would have. Thanks to you, Uncle D, I had a channel to Dierdorf and managed to get a message to him that he shouldn't show up."

"You do realize that you can't prove any of this, right?" DeHoic demanded.

"I'm not really in the proving things business, dumpling. Being a politician, I'm more in the shameless insinuation and underhanded manipulation business."

"So are we coming to the underhanded manipulation part?" DeHoic sounded like she'd gotten pretty much all of her piss and vinegar back.

"Uh huh." I bent over and picked up the thumb-drive. "I strongly suspect that this is a plant and that you planted it. I know companies make bedframes with hidden compartments where guys can hide pot and coke and porn from their wives and their kids—but the police know about that too. No way a crime-scene search in a high-profile murder investigation missed that secret drawer. Whatever is on here, you put it there, planning to use me as a cut-out to get it to the police without any record of your involvement."

"Get to the manipulation stuff," DeHoic said, "because this background is pretty boring."

"The most logical explanation for the murder is that Dierdorf got wind that Jerzy had targeted him and did unto Jerzy before Jerzy could do unto him."

"So what?"

"So if it should somehow get back to Dierdorf that you were shopping around a database that you said would compromise him, his reaction would be predictable, don't you think?"

DeHoic glared at Klimchock.

"Did Dierdorf send you here?"

"Nope." Klimchock shared a cheery smile with us. "I warned him off and that was it. He did mention to me that you'd said you'd leave the front door open for him—thanks very much—but no way he was coming. I'm an entrepreneur, though. I thought if there was something here that he might find it useful to know, he'd be grateful if I got it for him. We know from scripture that we are not to bury our talents but to multiply them tenfold. Matthew, Chapter twenty-five, verses fourteen to thirty."

"If this thumb-drive ends up in brother Klimchock's hands, Ms. DeHoic," I said, "the way I see things you would only have one real good option: have your shyster go to the FBI with whatever information potentially incriminating Dierdorf you have, and let the Feds take it from there. Immunity shouldn't be much of a problem. I can guarantee you the FBI wants him more than it wants you."

DeHoic's face paled. There's fear and then there's FEAR, the kind you can smell, that makes you sick to your stomach. I sensed the second kind oozing out of her. She took a couple of breaths, though, and when she spoke she did it in a calm voice with only a little edge to it.

"Now listen to me. Carefully. This isn't a game. We're not talking about getting some in-bred halfwit elected to Congress from Lickspittle, Mississippi. This is real life about real people with real guns—and if you give that thumb-drive to this Bible-thumping yahoo to pass on to Dierdorf, you will have real blood on your hands."

"As long as it isn't my blood, darlin', I have no problem with that."

"That's my girl." Uncle D said that with lip-smacking pride.

Chapter Fifty-one

On my way back I managed to reach Tony and tell him to go ahead and sign off on the plea bargain. After all, a deal's a deal. I even remembered to throw in *pas de merde* so that he'd know the message was genuine.

After that, things went downhill. The adrenaline rush from the fight and the aftermath had run dry, so the delayed reaction from the punishment I'd absorbed set in. My nose had been hurting since DeHoic had pasted me with that gun in her paw, but now it dialed the hurt up a couple of notches. I suddenly noticed that I had to squint to make out the numbers on my dashboard. Started feeling a little woozy, and even thought I might toss my cookies. No way I could gut this out all the way back to D.C. Fortunately, Siri came up with a regional medical center less than ten miles farther on. I made it, but not by any large margin.

After-Action Assessment of the Damage Control Strategy

Chapter Fifty-two

I figured I'd have to wait forever in the emergency room, but one good look at me and the admitting nurse said something about "stat" into a loudspeaker as soon as she'd photocopied my insurance card. Next thing I knew I was lying in a bed and a resident was talking to me about surgery. Concussion; broken nose; hairline fracture in the bone around my right eye; and blood leaking into the socket. I told him to track down a surgeon without waiting for any paint to dry.

When I woke up I saw Rafe sitting beside my bed. I tried to start an explanation that wouldn't sound too idiotic, but he gently shushed me. I was so spaced out on painkillers that I would have had trouble making any sense anyway.

Speaking of painkillers, it beats me how people can get addicted to them. Wallowing in a gauzy cocoon where you feel like you're only about half there, can't read, can't think quick or clearly, can't say anything smart—if that's your idea of high, I'll take normal, thank you very much.

Sometime Saturday afternoon I started to come out of it enough to check my iPad, but I just picked up little scraps of news and gossip. The only one I remember is that Theo McAbbott was getting some buzz, what with his second book showing up twenty feet from *Marine One*. Recapitulations of reviews for that book and his first one and, of course, courtesy of Rafe, jabbering about the one he had in the pipeline—which was suddenly "much anticipated."

Rafe sat by me every blessed waking second. Seamus came by on Saturday. Very upbeat about the NRA thing, but I could tell from his face that he was worried sick. He was absolutely convinced that making me a YouTube star was what had somehow gotten me beaten up. Told me to take the next couple of weeks off. The box of chocolates he brought me came from the hospital gift shop, but it's the thought that counts.

They finally discharged me Sunday morning. Rafe drove me home. I felt pretty clear-headed by then, especially because I'd made it a point to get by without Percocet since Saturday afternoon. Aches and pains, of course, but nothing migraine-level in my head and the mouse around my eye had shrunk quite a bit. I felt like I could finally explain how I'd ended up on the casualty list.

"You're probably wondering what the Hell happened to me."

"I have a pretty good idea what the Hell happened to you, Josephine Robideaux Kendall. I had a little wink-wink, nudge-nudge talk with your uncle."

"Oh."

"Uncle Darius was a bit vague about whether you'd gotten what you came for *chez* Schroeder," Rafe said then. "Did you?"

"Only time will tell for sure—and I have no idea how long it will take."

"As my wife sometimes says, that doesn't come as a complete surprise."

"Okay, then." I took a good breath and squared my shoulders. "Now, Rafe Kendall, I think you have a thing or two you might want to share with me."

"When we land," he said.

"When we land? Land where?"

"Paris. You're young and resilient, so today, Monday, and Tuesday should be enough time for you to rest up, and you won't need more than a couple of hours to pack. We have first-class tickets on Air France leaving from Dulles on Wednesday evening. Lie-flat seats, so we'll be able to sleep on the flight.

Even with a shiner, you'll still be the most beautiful woman in Paris. As soon as we land, I'll answer every question you have."

Paris. Whoa!

Rafe nailed it on my bounce-back. By the time we went to bed Monday night I'd say I was up to eighty percent, and by Tuesday afternoon if it weren't for the bandages and a bit of colorful swelling around my eye, you wouldn't know anything unusual had happened to me.

We hadn't even left for Paris yet, much less landed there, so we didn't talk about my questions and Rafe's explanations while we shared a little snack in his home-office around three p.m. on Tuesday. Instead, we talked about Ann DeHoic.

"I think she's even smarter than Jerzy was," I mused. "And she's as ruthless as they come. But she just doesn't have his instincts, his natural feel for the scam, the sheer joy he took in putting together a caper. When she tried to pull off the hustle herself instead of just helping him do it, she got in way over her head."

"Thank God for that. If she'd had better criminal instincts, you might be dead."

"You're right. I won the fight, but I still ended up in the hospital—and I'm not sure she got much more than a headache out of it. She was a lot stronger than I thought she'd be."

"She was stronger but you were tougher. You had the guts to step in and take her last punch, even though you knew it'd hurt like Hell, because you figured it would open her up to a counter-punch that would end the fight. Which it did. You had a rough weekend, but you came out of it okay."

I had a rough month, buddy, not just a rough weekend. But maybe that's what it took for me to grow up. I'm not a moral adolescent anymore.

Didn't say any of that because Rafe's sententiousness threshold is even lower than mine. I thought it, though. I was still running it through my head when the phone rang. After glancing at the caller-ID screen, Rafe mouthed "lawyer" at me and answered.

"Hey, Mike. Josie is here with me. I'm going to put you on speaker."

"Get CNN on the biggest computer screen you have. Click the arrow on the lead video."

Rafe complied. Glued to the grainy digital footage that started streaming, I only half-registered words at the bottom: "Breaking News…FBI tapes just released…Fleeing fugitive." Shot through the windshield of a trailing car, the video showed a black SUV rumbling down a narrow, paved strip in otherwise open country. Ahead of it, a Gulfstream jet chugged down the macadam, looking like it was desperately trying to pick up speed. The SUV seemed to gain for a moment, then fell farther back. A stand of pine trees at the end of the runway seemed terrifyingly close. The jet got its wheels off the ground and started to climb, but not quite fast enough. Part of the landing gear caught on a treetop. The jet cartwheeled through the air over the pine, out of sight beyond the tree line. Flames bursting upward well above the treetops, though, sent an unmistakable message: crashed and burned.

"Dierdorf?" Rafe asked.

"So they say. Got an unexpected visit from the FBI and decided to run for it. Didn't have enough runway for a proper takeoff and either took a chance or decided too late to abort. Either way, you only make that mistake once."

"I'm guessing they'll stamp 'SOLVED' on the Jerzy Schroeder case now," Rafe said.

"They almost have to. You can't indict a corpse, even in Maryland. I mean, only a paid Dierdorf hit-man could plausibly have murdered Schroeder, right?"

"Works for me."

"They'll grill the Hell out of Reuter. He'll say he didn't do it. They'll say, 'Then who did?' And he'll either keep his mouth shut, which will make him look as guilty as Hell, or throw some recently deceased Dierdorf thug under the bus. If he has trouble coming up with a thug who died with Dierdorf in the plane crash, they might give him a hint. Either way, case closed."

"Primo analytics," Rafe said. "Thanks for calling."

"Always glad to be the bearer of good news. By the way. Fella named Danny Klimchock called. Said he has an intuition that the Department of Energy may shift Dierdorf's solar power subsidy to another solar power company that will require some applied engineering services from Klimchock. Figures a Washington lawyer might prove helpful. No ethical conflict that I can see, but would that raise any kind of client relations concern on your part?"

"Nope. Full speed ahead, take no prisoners."

"Thanks."

Rafe clicked the phone off and turned toward me, smiling like a sales rep who'd just snagged the Coors concession on fraternity row at LSU.

"I guess you did get what you came for at Schroeder's house."

"Copy that, tiger."

Chapter Fifty-three

I didn't start on Rafe the moment we put round rubber down at Charles de Gaulle International Airport outside Paris. I waited until we'd checked into Le Tremoille near the Champs Elysées and unpacked and gotten a five-star brunch delivered by room service. *Then* I teed off.

"All right. I've got this much. You knew right from the git-go that something didn't smell right about Jerzy Schroeder coming to a raw rookie like me to handle his Dierdorf project. You turned to McAbbott, who found out from friends he still has at the Bureau that Dierdorf was both big-time bad news and Jerzy's current target of opportunity. So you hired McAbbott to flesh that out with his own surveillance efforts. He came through with the picture of Jerzy's ex next to Dierdorf and a couple of shady characters tied to a Jerzy scam."

"You figured all that out by yourself? You're a pretty smart girl."

"Not as smart as you. Once you'd put those pieces together, you realized that Jerzy planned to kill me and frame Dierdorf for the murder, because the only way I could realistically help him pull off a subsidy swap was by providing a convenient corpse. So you had someone forge a bill of sale showing that you'd gotten rid of your hunting rifle years ago, even though you still had it. Who handled the forgery, by the way?"

"Well, if there were a forgery, it would be deliciously ironic if Schroeder had arranged it—in exchange, say, for inside information about Dierdorf."

"From McAbbott."

"I suppose so, if you want to speculate."

"You bought a telescopic sight for the rifle, had it expertly mounted, and did some target practice at a gun store well outside the area. You paid cash for a pair of shoes that you'd get rid of after you wore them the day you killed Jerzy. You hoped the Feds would moot Jerzy's whole plan by arresting Dierdorf, but they didn't move fast enough. When we were talking during our run a couple of days after the murder, you unintentionally let slip that you thought Jerzy was taking me to a meeting with Dierdorf. You had that thought because McAbbott told you that Jerzy had generated documentation supposedly showing that Dierdorf would be in the area that day. When you learned that, you knew Jerzy was about to take me out and you couldn't wait any longer. Leaving your cell phone with McAbbott at his place, you hustled out to Jerzy's house the day Dierdorf would supposedly be in D.C., perched in a tree at the back of the property, and ambushed Jerzy when he came out of the house with me. You committed cold-blooded murder to save my life."

"Did I now?"

"Yes, you did."

"And how did I get McAbbott to go along with all this felonious behavior without paying him a huge amount of money—which a comprehensive forensic audit has shown I didn't do?"

"You offered him something worth much more than money to an author: sizzle and the promise of celebrity and fame. One-moment-in-time stuff. Book events with lines stretching out the front doors and way down the sidewalks at Barnes and Nobles in twenty cities. You pulled strings and called in chits and did favors and asked for favors until you got a shot of a senior aide carrying *Knuckle Rap* while she was walking behind the President of the United States. Things you ordinarily wouldn't have done for any client of yours short of an ex-Secretary of State. Suddenly McAbbott's upcoming thriller is big-time Beltway buzz-bait. Every paper that matters will review it and two or three will do profiles of him. Amazon will have to lay on extra staff just to cover the pre-orders. Most authors would kill for that. McAbbott only had to help you kill—and then back up your alibi to the hilt. The only thing I can't figure out is how you kept the cops from finding the serial number of your rifle when they did the infrared trick."

"Hypothetically, you mean."

"Fuck hypothetically."

"Well, your buddies at the NRA have fixed things so that anyone willing to attend a gun show can buy a rifle without proving his identity, going through a background check, or using a credit card, as long as there are sellers there who aren't federally licensed firearms dealers—and there always are. Completely anonymous transactions. So, hypothetically, I could have just bought another Winchester three-oh-eight, machined off the serial number, used my own rifle for the execution—or what you for some reason keep calling the murder—and left the gun-show rifle I'd bought for the police to find. Raising the serial number would confirm that it wasn't mine, giving the police one more reason to drop me from the suspect list."

"But ballistics would show that that rifle wasn't the murder weapon."

"Ballistics is only an exact science on television. If, hypothetically, the killer used a soft-nosed bullet that would split into lots of tiny fragments by the time it made the exit wound, proving anything with a ballistics test would be a pretty chancy proposition. And if the ballistics test did exclude the rifle they found, that would just be one more frustrating dead end for them. Hypothetically."

"So you did it."

"That's a very creative conjecture on your part. But tell me this: if all of what you think you've figured out were true, how would you feel about it?"

I don't think he really had to ask. I'll give you eight to one he could pick up my vibe without any verbal hints from me. I took a deep, cleansing breath, though, told myself to relax, and answered his question.

"Well, I hate to traffic in gender stereotypes, but we modern, twenty-first century women aren't hung up on intellectual or emotional consistency. We want men who are polite and thoughtful and considerate and generous lovers and respectful of our intellects and who love us for ourselves alone, *et cetera*. That's what we love. But while we're loving all that stuff—well, bad boys turn us on. Big time. And it doesn't get badder than slaying a dragon for us when we're in distress."

"Even if it's not a fair fight?"

"What were you supposed to do? Try to follow Jerzy and me and wait until he had the gun to my head before you shot him? Dragons don't fight fair. From a strictly bad-ass point of view, they don't deserve an even break."

"So you get a kick out of vibrating to the shivering thrill of dangerous company at eleven o'clock in the morning?" Rafe asked.

"Yeah—or pretty much any other time."

That tore it. Rafe and I started playing all our favorite Washington bedroom games from our first few months together: Majority Whip; Discharge Petition; Naughty Intern; Motion to Table; Binding Resolution; and Monica's First Cigar. We didn't leave the room for three days.

I was afraid Rafe might overdo it a bit on Naughty Intern. I'd decided that if he did, I'd know where he was coming from so I'd just suck it up and take it. He didn't, though. Overdo it, I mean. Much. Partly he's a real gentleman, and partly I laid on the Creole charm with a trowel, and partly I just plain wore him out.

I guess by then I'd gotten real good at damage control.

To receive a free catalog of Poisoned Pen Press titles, please
provide your name, address, and e-mail address in one of the
following ways:

Phone: 1-800-421-3976
Facsimile: 1-480-949-1707
Email: info@poisonedpenpress.com
Website: www.poisonedpenpress.com

Poisoned Pen Press
6962 E. First Ave. Ste 103
Scottsdale, AZ 85251